FALLEN OAKS

The second novel in the Blue Water
historical mystery series

James P. Maywar

iUniverse, Inc.
New York Lincoln Shanghai

Fallen Oaks

The second novel in the Blue Water historical mystery series

Copyright © 2006 by James P. Mayar

iUniverse books may be ordered through booksellers or by contacting:

iUniverse
2021 Pine Lake Road, Suite 100
Lincoln, NE 68512
www.iuniverse.com
1-800-Authors (1-800-288-4677)

This is a work of fiction. All of the characters, names, incidents, organizations, and dialogue in this novel are either the products of the author's imagination or are used fictitiously.

ISBN: 978-0-595-42050-6 (pbk)
ISBN: 978-0-595-86395-2 (ebk)

Printed in the United States of America

For my sons, Eric and Drew, and
their lovely wives, Donna and Rie.
No father could be more fortunate.

Acknowledgments

Within this book, most of the information about the United States in 1919 came from the following sources: *Henry Ford and the Jews: The Mass Production of Hate* by Neil Baldwin, *The Great Influenza: The Epic Story of the Deadliest Plague in History* by John M. Barry, *Bound for Canaan: The Underground Railroad and the War for the Soul of America* by Fergus M. Bordewich, *The Negro Leagues Book* edited by Dick Clark and Larry Lester, *American Costume, 1915–1970* by Shirley Miles O'Donnol, and *The Fiery Cross: Ku Klux Klan in America* by Wyn Craig Wade.

Most of the information about Port Huron, Michigan, during the same year came from the following sources: 1919 issues of the *Port Huron Times Herald,* the Michigan Room of the St. Clair County Library, *Tunnel Tales* by Wanda Pratt, *From Whence We Came* by Marguerite Stanley, and *An Enduring Heritage* by Keith Yates.

The iUniverse editor did another excellent job.

Patsy Chapman, Ed Fitzgerald, Bob Irving, George Joachim, Wendy Krabach, and reference librarians at the St. Clair County Library and the Michigan Law Library helped me with my research.

George and Sharon Joachim, Eric Maywar, and Catherine and Ed Moore read the first draft and offered helpful suggestions.

My wonderful wife, Nancy, read several drafts and provided enthusiastic support.

PROLOGUE

───────────── ▼ ─────────────

Fall 1919

Bill Boyd strolled into the train's club car and found a seat near the rear. He sat down, stretched his legs, and crossed them at the ankles. Bill had boarded the train in Philadelphia early that morning and was scheduled to arrive in Ann Arbor, Michigan, by nine o'clock that night.

A Negro waiter appeared at his side almost immediately. "I'd like a bottle of beer," Bill said. The waiter nodded and headed off toward the kitchen.

As he waited for his drink to arrive, Bill began to daydream. His mind took him through the series of events that had led to his boarding of the train. When the United States entered the Great War, the government proceeded to draft all single men between the ages of twenty-one and thirty. Bill had been thirty. He decided that rather than waiting to be drafted, he would enlist. As a college graduate, he was commissioned a lieutenant in the army. When the government realized he had eight years experience working for his uncle as a reporter in Port Huron, Michigan, Bill was assigned to the Committee on Public Information and was stationed in Philadelphia.

After Bill's discharge in March 1919, he decided to stay in Philadelphia, where he landed a job as a reporter at the *Public Ledger*. Bill was not sure he would ever return to Port Huron, but a phone call he'd received a week ago had changed his plans.

His uncle, Clayton Boyd, had suffered a heart attack and wanted Bill to return home to operate the newspaper while he recuperated. Clayton's doctor had recommended three months rest, and Bill had agreed to return for those three months. He hoped his obligation to his uncle would be over within that period of time so he could return to Philadelphia. In the meantime, he decided to take advantage of his return to Port Huron, by taking a detour to his alma mater in Ann Arbor to attend the Michigan vs. Ohio State football game.

As he thought about the joy of watching Michigan play its main rival, the waiter returned with his beer. Bill smiled grimly, knowing that in less than three months, alcohol would no longer be sold legally in the United States. Many states, including Michigan and Ohio, had already banned the sale of alcohol. Bill wondered how many fans at the football game would be sneaking flasks into the stadium. He looked out the window and saw his gray suit and purple bow tie reflected in the glass. He lifted the beer and offered a silent toast. *To prohibition—America's great folly.*

Bill took a sip of beer and began reading *The Four Horsemen of the Apocalypse* by Vicente Blasco Ibanez, the top-selling novel in the United States. After reading several pages he placed the book on his lap and stared out the window. To his regret, he was unable to rid his mind of the imagery of the four horsemen—Pestilence, War, Famine, and Death.

The first rider was Pestilence astride a white horse. In 1918 and 1919, Pestilence appeared in the form of the great influenza pandemic. The virus arrived on the east coast of the United States in the fall of 1918 with a vengeance. Bill remembered how terrifying it had been in Philadelphia. When more than one hundred people died in the first two days of October, the city banned all public meetings. Churches, schools, theaters, even public funerals were closed. But it seemed to do little good.

During the height of the pandemic, Bill contacted Lieutenant Commander R. W. Plummer, chief health officer for the Philadelphia Naval District, to arrange a visit to a hospital facility. He regretted that visit. Men were placed in a converted gymnasium, their cots so close together they were almost elbow to elbow. Blood was everywhere. It came from soldiers' noses, ears, and lungs. Bill still had nightmares about that visit.

Moving on, Bill reflected on the second horseman of the apocalypse, War, riding a red horse. The Great War began in 1914 and ravaged the world for five long years. Modern equipment, such as tanks, airplanes, poison gas, and submarines made this war different from its predecessors. Trench warfare magnified the brutality of this conflict.

Bill supported the idea that civilians needed to sacrifice during a war, so he did not find the concepts of "meatless Tuesday" and "wheatless Wednesday" objectionable. But it concerned him greatly when people were pressured to be patriotic. In April 1918, St. Clair County, Michigan, had a Liberty Bond campaign. The Liberty Loan Committee decided that when someone refused to give what was considered a fair share, a card would be completed and placed on file. Local newspapers quoted committeemen as saying, "when the big war fund drive is over, the committee expects to have complete data on every family in St. Clair County. It will be of great assistance in listing citizens as loyal or disloyal."

The war ended in 1918, but Europe's problems were not over. The third horseman, Famine, mounted on a black horse, rode across the war-ravaged land. Bill recalled that the shortage of food in many European countries, particularly Germany, was severe. It was estimated that Germany needed at least two hundred thousand tons of wheat each month to avoid starvation.

As the countryside passed outside the window, Bill watched several horses peacefully grazing. He imagined a meeting between the four horsemen.

Pestilence, War, and Famine are assembled waiting for the fourth member of their group. Riding a pale horse, Death moves swiftly to join them. The three horses facing Death pull back their lips. With their teeth showing, they appear to be sneering.

Disappointment is evident in Famine's voice. "Only a few million people starved to death in Europe. The success of the relief efforts managed to keep the number lower than I had expected."

War brandishes a blood-soaked sword and shouts, "I am pleased to report that eighteen million soldiers and civilians died between 1914 and 1918."

But it is Pestilence who has the most astonishing report. Smirking at the relatively small numbers mentioned by the first two riders, he says, "Over fifty million people died as a result of the influenza pandemic of 1918 and 1919."

Death accepts each report with a slight nod. He then turns and rides away.

Bill stared at the book on his lap. He looked up to see the Negro waiter doing his job quickly and efficiently. It occurred to him that a fifth horseman, Racial Hatred, should be considered. This horseman would ride a multicolored horse that would constantly bite itself to illustrate that racial hatreds are self-destructive.

In 1919, the United States was experiencing a period of intense hatred toward blacks, Catholics, Jews, and immigrants. Bill was not one to wallow in negativity, but he was saddened by the recent outbreak of lynchings and race riots.

Bill waved to the waiter. "I would like another beer."

"Sorry. I can't sell any more liquor because we will be entering Ohio in a few minutes."

"Would it be possible to have a cup of coffee, or have they outlawed caffeine too?"

The waiter smiled. "Coffee is still legal."

Bill tossed *The Four Horsemen of Apocalypse* on the table and looked at its cover. He wondered how much the war had changed him because he knew that a few years ago; one of the riders would have been Lady Godiva in her resplendent nakedness.

CHAPTER 1

▼

Eight-year-old Amanda Sharpe bounded down the steps of James K. Polk School and headed for her grandmother's house. Amanda was excited. She had earned a small part in a community play called *Two Families—One America.* The cast had been practicing for nearly a month, and opening night was only one week away. Her grandmother was making her costume.

The production was being directed by Clara Sibella and was being presented at the Majestic Theater in downtown Port Huron. Sibella directed many community plays, including *The Imaginary Invalid,* performed in 1918 as a benefit for the war effort.

Amanda's role was to play the young daughter in a family that had lived in the United States for several generations. Her family was forced to face a challenge when an immigrant family from Italy moved in next door. Amanda had overheard the older actors referring to the play as a commentary on prejudice and discrimination. She didn't understand exactly what they meant, but it didn't matter to her. She simply enjoyed performing.

Skipping most of the way to her grandmother's house, her auburn pigtails swaying back and forth, she quickly covered the three blocks from her school. Amanda swung the front door open. "Grandma, I'm here!"

Gladys Sharpe, a stout, gray-haired woman in her mid-fifties smiled. "And as full of energy as ever, I see."

Amanda dashed into the kitchen. "May I have some milk and cookies before we start? I'm starved."

"You know where they are. Help yourself while I get your costume."

Gladys carried the costume and a sewing basket to a chair she had placed in the middle of the living room. Amanda plopped onto the sofa, munched on a chocolate chip cookie, and looked at the flowered wallpaper. "Gee Grandma, the new wallpaper looks swell."

Gladys sat down beside Amanda. "Thank you. Your grandpa and I were really tired when we finished. I think we're getting too old for this kind of work."

"Maybe I could help next time."

Gladys smiled. "That would be nice. Now tell me how the rehearsals are going."

"Wonderful. Miss Sibella is great and I met a new friend. Her name is Rosa Campanella."

"Is Rosa an Italian?"

Amanda leaned her head against the large doily on the sofa as she chewed her cookie. "Yes. Which is just perfect, because she plays an Italian in the play."

Gladys asked, "Why didn't you know her before?"

"She goes to Catholic school."

"I see. Have you learned all your words for the play?"

Amanda finished her milk and set the glass down on the coffee table. "They're called lines, Grandma. And I've learned them all. Do you want to hear?"

Before Gladys could respond, Amanda jumped up and assumed a theatrical pose. In a loud voice, she said, "Mommy, may I play with the new neighbor girl? I just found out we're the same age."

Gladys's hand flew to her chest. "Goodness me, that was loud!" she said, a bit shocked.

"I'm following Miss Sibella's instructions. She said that instead of minding their p's and q's, actors should mind their p's and a's. That stands for projection … and a big word I can't pronounce."

"Do you mean articulation?"

"That's the word. It means to speak clearly."

Gladys laughed. "I think you minded your p's and a's well. Are you ready to try on your costume?"

"Yes!" Amanda grabbed the costume and dashed off to the bedroom. Minutes later, she returned smiling. "Oh, Grandma, it's beautiful." She twirled around the room in a light blue pleated skirt and a white sailor blouse with dark trim.

Gladys hugged her granddaughter. "You're the one who is beautiful." Releasing her hold, she said, "Now stand on that chair, and I'll adjust the length of the skirt."

As Gladys pinned the hemline, she said, "I understand you are now a member of the Order of the Rose." The Order of the Rose was an organization for girls, age five to sixteen, sponsored by the Woman's Benefit Association.

Amanda asked, "Were you in the Order of the Rose when you were my age?"

"No, honey. They didn't have it when I was a girl. But I know a lot about it."

"Like what?"

Gladys thought for a moment. "Well, let's see. I know the Order of the Rose teaches girls how to keep records, handle money, and conduct meetings."

"That's right, Grandma. I'm going to learn a lot of good things."

Gladys smiled as she continued to hem the dress. As recently as five years ago she would not have approved of such an organization. She felt that a woman's role should be limited to family and church. In 1913 when Michigan had a referendum on women's suffrage for the state, Mrs. Sharpe had talked her husband into voting against it.

Her opinions had changed somewhat when she saw how effectively women had taken over jobs during the war, but she still felt that certain distinctions between men's roles and women's roles should be maintained.

Amanda said, "I had fun in the Order of the Rose meetings this summer. Two young ladies, Miss Wendy and Miss Donna, taught many of the classes."

Gladys placed another pin in Amanda's skirt. "Who are they?"

"They're college students at MAC."

"Do you mean Michigan Agricultural College?"

Amanda nodded. "They made us laugh a lot, but Miss Wendy told us the skills we were learning would be important to us when we get older."

"That sounds like good advice."

"One day, Miss Donna entertained us with her trombone. She played jazz." Amanda shot her right arm in the air, simulating the motion of a slide trombone.

Gladys dropped her pincushion. "For goodness sakes girl, don't move like that. I nearly messed up your hem. And if you're not careful, you'll scratch your legs," she said as she retrieved her pincushion. "This Miss Donna actually played jazz at an Order of the Rose meeting?" Playing jazz was one of those "roles" Grandma Sharpe thought should be left to the men.

Amanda continued talking, unmindful of the discomfort she was causing her grandmother. "Yes. Then last week Sylvia Pointe talked about her experiences as a member of the Red Cross Motor Corps during the war."

Gladys stood up quickly, shocked by the fact that Sylvia Pointe would have been allowed to speak to young, impressionable children. When Sylvia worked as a secretary at the Port Huron Police Department, she'd had the nerve to ask that she be given a job as a regular policewoman. Mrs. Sharpe thought the idea of a policewoman was ridiculous. She breathed deeply a few times to regain her composure. "You can take your skirt off now. I'll have it ready by Sunday."

"Thanks, Grandma. May I have another cookie?"

"Of course."

Amanda climbed down from the chair and headed for the bedroom. The young girl failed to notice that Gladys was shaking her head and muttering about the need for women to be respectable.

*   *   *   *

Patrolman Tobias "Toby" Sharpe sat in his car near Pine Grove Park as he looked across the St. Clair River and watched the lights began to flicker on in Sarnia, Ontario. Toby, a stocky man with dark wavy hair and brown eyes, looked at his watch, took another long drink from his flask, and decided it was time to pick up his family.

He started his 1917 Model T, and drove carefully up Gratiot Avenue toward Holland Avenue. Minutes later he parked on the edge of Lakeside Cemetery near the memorial to the U.S. soldiers who died during a cholera epidemic in 1832. Army troops were moving westward to participate in the Black Hawk War when several soldiers contracted cholera. They were brought to Fort Gratiot for medical care. Unfortunately the epidemic spread among the soldiers at the fort.

Toby got out of his car, walked to the memorial, and read what he thought was an oddly phrased dedication. "To the memory of the U.S. Soldiers buried in these grounds, among those whose graves cannot be identified are they whose names are inscribed herein who fell victim to the cholera epidemic July 4 to 18, 1832." He remembered that the reason many of the soldiers could not be identified was that their bodies were never found. Suffering from high fever, many stripped off their clothes, jumped into Lake Huron, and drowned.

He pulled his heavy cardigan tighter and turned away from the memorial. A sudden gust of wind swirled dead oak leaves as he walked slowly to the grave site where his wife and son were working. His daughter, Natalie Sharpe, was one of thirty people in Port Huron who had died of influenza during the winter of 1918–1919. Natalie was born in the summer of 1916 and died in January 1919, a few months after the Great War ended.

Toby remembered how the war had changed the relationship between his wife, Mary, and his mother. Prior to the war, the two didn't get along. Mary's ideas about women's rights irritated his mother. During the war, while the older children, Chris and Amanda were at school, Toby's mother, wife, and youngest child went to the Woman's Benefit Association building where the Red Cross made triangular bandages, sweaters, mufflers, socks, towels, and surgical dressings for American soldiers.

Mary had stopped taking her daughter to public places when the influenza epidemic began in the spring of 1918. Sadly, this precaution did not prevent Natalie from contracting the illness. Her remains shared the same resting place as soldiers who'd surrendered their lives to the cholera epidemic nearly one hundred years earlier.

The war improved the relationship between Mary Sharpe and her mother-in-law. Unfortunately, Natalie's death created a negative change for Toby and his wife. Toby believed he had provided Mary with support, but he felt that everything he suggested to help minimize her sadness was rejected. To him, Mary seemed mired in depression, and he could do nothing about it. He had learned that stopping to sip whiskey at Pine Grove Park after work helped prepare him for the unhappy atmosphere at home.

Toby stood behind the two figures working diligently around the grave site. He looked at Mary's beautiful auburn hair and remembered how wonderful their relationship had been. His best friend, Bill Boyd, had commented several times about how impressed he was with Toby's marriage. He wondered what Bill might think the next time they saw each other. He thought, *Maybe it's better if Bill stays in Philadelphia rather than seeing how things are now.*

Toby walked closer. He said, "It looks nice."

Mary did not turn around. "Thanks."

Ten-year-old Chris, sensing the tension, looked at his parents. "Hi, Dad. We also cleaned the area next to Natalie. It seems like no one ever takes care of it properly."

Toby looked where Chris was pointing. He thought, *Natalie's area will be the cleanest in the cemetery if Mary has anything to do with it.* "It was nice you came along to help your mother," he said.

After placing her garden tools in a basket, Mary stood up and rubbed her lower back. Then she put her arm around Chris and said, "Yes. He is quite a good helper."

Chris said, "Golly, this is easy compared to the war garden contest that I entered last year. Remember how the bank gave me free garden seeds and a booklet on gardening?"

Mary nodded, "We were so proud when you won a bronze medal for having one of the ten best-looking gardens in the city."

Toby agreed, "You certainly learned some good skills last year."

Chris asked, "Remember how Natalie used to compare herself to the height of the corn stalks? And how she cried when the corn stalks got taller that she was?"

Mary and Toby stared at each other. Toby reached over and took the basket Mary was holding. "I think it's time to go home. Amanda should be ready to be picked up."

Mary said, "Just a minute," as she used her shoe to remove a few newly fallen oak leaves from Natalie's grave. She stood in silence for a few minutes, her head bowed. She raised her head. "It's time to go. We don't want Amanda spoiling her supper with too many of Grandma's cookies."

CHAPTER 2

▼

Russell Wilcox carried four two-by-fours and placed them in a horse-drawn wagon. He removed his gloves and took an order form from the chest pocket of his bib overalls. He carefully compared it to the lumber he had collected. Russell was the only black employee at Stockwell's Lumber Company. He felt it especially important that he not make mistakes. He knew that many of the white customers, as well as some of his fellow employees, would not hesitate to complain to Mr. Stockwell.

Russell smiled politely to the customer. "Looks like we had everything you wanted, Mr. Bannister. This will make a fine rabbit hutch. If you don't mind my asking, where are you going to keep it?"

"It's going to be in my garage." Mr. Bannister chuckled, "I'm going to start with four rabbits. Who knows how many I'll have by next summer."

"They'll sure make some good eatin'."

"I just hope our kids don't get too attached to them. They've already picked out names, and we don't even have the rabbits yet."

"Thanks for your business, and be sure to come back if you need anything else."

Mr. Bannister climbed up on the wagon and gently flicked the reins on the horse's backside. Tiger, a large yellow cat, ran out from between the wheels and followed Russell as the young man walked to the office to see if there were more orders to fill.

Russell was twenty years old, medium height, and wiry. A first impression would suggest that he was athletic, but a one-inch sole on his left shoe, necessary to correct a birth defect, required a reassessment. His deformity and skin color made him doubly vulnerable to harassment when he was in school. Some of the students had called him, "Stepin' Fetchit."

Mrs. Stockwell looked up when Russell entered the office. "All the orders have been filled, but Mr. Stockwell wants to see you for a minute," she said.

"Yes, ma'am." He walked to Mr. Stockwell's private office and knocked on the door.

Mr. Stockwell, a tall, thin man with unruly red hair, waved him into the office. He pointed at a chair. "Come on in and take a load off."

After Russell was seated, Mr. Stockwell asked, "Well, Russell, how long have you worked here?"

"If you count the time I worked summers while I was in high school, it's been five years."

"That's what my wife told me this morning. We think you're entitled to another raise." He looked at a ledger on his desk, and continued, "Mrs. Stockwell's record book shows that you're now earning sixty-five cents an hour. What do you think about an increase to seventy-five cents?"

Russell said, "Thank you, Mr. Stockwell. You sure are generous. If I work fifty hours a week like always, that'll bring my wages to $37.50."

The two men stood and shook hands. "I like to reward hard workers. I don't want you finding another job that pays better."

Russell grinned. "You don't have to worry about that."

"Good. Now you go on home, and say hello to your mother."

The Stockwells watched Russell leave the office as Mrs. Stockwell put her arm around her husband's waist. "You sure like that young man, don't you?"

"Yep. He's always been polite and hardworking. I'd consider making him a foreman someday if I thought the other workers would accept him."

*   *   *   *

Four of the lumberyard's employees—Boone Eckard, Hank Peters, Lester Johnson, and Harry Moss—also watched as Russell left the office. Boone spit a stream of tobacco juice as he asked, "What's that darky doin' in Stockwell's office?"

Harry threw a stone at Tiger who was lying in the shade nearby. He then asked sarcastically, "How do you think he got that brown nose?"

Tiger watched the stone fly over his head, turned, and stared at the four men.

Lester laughed. "You better be careful, Harry. That mangy cat might put a mouse in your lunch pail."

Hank said, "I heard Stockwell's goin' to give Russell a raise."

Boone sneered. "That coon better not get too big for his britches or we're going to have to do something about him." Boone stood and scratched his backside. "Don't forget the poker game at my house Saturday. Be there by six. I got plenty of hard cider, so you'll have something to make you feel good when you lose."

*   *   *   *

Russell hurried home thinking about the pay raise. He and Lillie Mae Grant were planning to get married next summer and the additional money would be helpful. He passed Oscar's Grocery Store and waved at the owner, Oscar Danbridge, who was sweeping the sidewalk out front.

Oscar, a large black man with a bushy mustache, waved back. "You be sure to bring your momma to church Sunday."

Russell continued walking. "I will; promise."

Moments later a carload of white men drove past Russell. One passenger shouted an obscenity and threw a beer bottle in his direction. Russell ducked as it flew by, hit a tree, and shattered into hundreds of pieces. He stood still for what seemed like an eternity as the car slowly came to a stop.

The driver got out and shook his fist at Russell who turned to run in the opposite direction. He stopped when he saw a passenger from the backseat get out of the car and run toward the driver.

The passenger yelled, "Mike, don't do this! Now ..." He stopped speaking as he grabbed Mike's arm. The passenger turned to see Oscar looking in their direction. When he continued his reprimand, it was with less volume. "Get back in the car."

Mike yelled, "Aw, Luke! You ain't much fun since the war!"

Keeping a tight grip on Mike's arm, Luke Laboy spoke quietly. "Maybe I just got a different idea of what's fun. Now get back behind the wheel and drive us back to the garage."

Russell waited until the car was out of sight before he continued home. He opened the door and yelled, "Momma, guess what?"

"Glory be. What's all the shoutin' about?"

"Mr. Stockwell gave me a raise. I'm now earnin' seventy-five cents an hour. I figured I'll be makin' about $1,900 next year."

Freeda Wilcox gave her son a big hug. "Well, I'm sure you're worth every penny. Now you get washed up for dinner. I've fixed ham, collard greens, and macaroni and cheese."

CHAPTER 3

▼

The Grand Trunk Railroad Depot was undoubtedly the most ornate building in Port Huron. Construction of the building began in 1891 to coincide with the opening of the St. Clair River Tunnel. Serving travelers since 1892, it was two stories high with a multicolored facade of brick and sandstone. The Grand Trunk Railroad had selected a Spanish Renaissance architectural style for the depot which included projecting pilasters and an overhanging slate roof.

After a fire in 1908 destroyed much of the interior, the building was refinished in cherry and ash. The first floor had two massive fireplaces, a waiting room, and a dining room. The second floor was made up of offices and storage rooms. Passengers using the depot were able to board trains that ran to three large cities—Detroit since 1859, and Chicago and Toronto since 1879.

Mary Sharpe, a short woman with a slight build, wore her beautiful auburn hair in a loose bun as she stood in front of the depot and waved good-bye to the family car as it disappeared. Mary walked inside and noticed that the chilly autumn morning had prompted the lighting of one of the depot's fireplaces. She took a seat near the blaze and enjoyed its warmth.

Mary's younger sister, Rebecca, had invited Mary to Detroit for a weekend visit to celebrate the older sibling's upcoming thirtieth birthday. Mary ordinarily took the interurban to Detroit because it was cheaper, but Rebecca had purchased the train ticket, perhaps as a way to insure Mary would make the trip. Mary did appreciate that the train was more comfortable and much faster than the interurban which was essentially a single street car without the comforts of a regular train. It took approximately two hours for the train to travel from Port Huron to Detroit while the interurban took nearly four hours.

The ticket master poked his head out of the ticket window. "The train for Detroit is now boarding."

Mary picked up her suitcase, boarded the train, and found a seat near a window. The train lurched forward and was soon running smoothly toward Detroit. When the conductor stopped in front of her, she handed him her ticket. He asked, "Going to Detroit by yourself, ma'am?"

"Yes. I'm spending the weekend with my sister."

"Are you planning to return Sunday morning?"

"Yes."

"Then I advise you to be at the station early. That train is often full."

"Thank you. I'll be sure to be there in plenty of time."

Relaxing to the rhythmic pattern of the train, Mary began to reflect on her current situation. She knew she was experiencing terrible sadness in the wake of her daughter's death, but she felt that her sadness mimicked the feelings of any parent who had lost a child. She could not understand why her husband did not seem to share her emotions. He never wanted to talk about Natalie's death, and he became upset when Mary sat beside Natalie's empty crib.

She knew she was less sad than she had been six months ago. On good days, when she was able to carry on as she did before the death, Toby would immediately assume she was done grieving. He would then become quietly angry when the sadness resurfaced.

She doubted she would ever be completely over the tragedy, and she felt that her husband was masking his true feelings. The fact that he often returned home from work with alcohol on his breath reinforced her belief that he was holding things inside. She knew that society pressured men to be strong and not to cry, but it still frustrated her that she and Toby were unable to talk openly about the effect Natalie's death was having on them.

She found many of her feelings were reflected in the book she was reading, *Winesburg, Ohio*, by Sherwood Anderson. In the chapter she was currently reading, the character Alice, overwhelmed with feelings of loss, ran naked in the rain. She knew Toby would have a difficult time understanding Alice's behavior, but she recognized that kind of desperation. Mary closed the book as tears began to fill her eyes.

Her thoughts were interrupted when the conductor announced, "Next stop, Oaks Corner."

Mary was surprised that the time had gone so quickly. The train was nearly halfway to Detroit. Looking out the window, she noticed that the buildings in

Oaks Corner were typical of most small towns adjacent to railroads. The town featured a church, a saloon, a grocery store, and a grain elevator.

The conductor noticed that Mary was crying and asked, "Are you OK, ma'am?"

She looked at his sympathetic expression and wiped her eyes. "I will be in a minute."

"Is there anything I can do? Would you like a glass of water?"

Mary shook her head. "No, I'm fine."

As Mary gazed out the window, a melancholy smile crossed her lips. She fingered the pages of *Winesburg, Ohio*, and thought, *Perhaps I need an adventure.*

＊　　　＊　　　＊　　　＊

Toby finished setting the table. "Time for lunch."

Amanda and Chris walked reluctantly to the kitchen. Chris asked, "What did you fix us?"

"Fried baloney-and-cheese sandwiches."

Chris turned to leave, but Amanda grabbed his arm. In a stage whisper, she said, "We both have to eat it."

Toby laughed. "I heard that. Sorry. I'm not a great chef, but it will fill your stomachs."

Chris groaned, "I'm afraid of what it will do *to* my stomach."

Amanda removed a blackened piece of meat from her sandwich and dropped it ceremoniously on her plate.

Noticing Amanda's behavior, Toby said, "Sorry. I burned part of the baloney." Changing the subject from comments about his inadequate cooking skills, he asked, "How is play practice going?"

Amanda chewed the rest of her sandwich quickly. "Great. Miss Sibella said she's sure we'll be ready for the opening performance next week. Mrs. Campanella is picking me up in about fifteen minutes."

Through a mouthful of sandwich, Chris asked, "Why are you going so early today?"

"There's some kind of special show tonight. We have to get out of the theater so they can set up."

Toby asked, "What do you do when you're not on the stage practicing?"

"I've been reading a book with the longest title I've ever seen. It's called *The Outdoor Girls in Army Service: Doing Their Bit for the Soldier Boys*. When I'm older, I want to have adventures and help people the way the outdoor girls do. So does Rosa."

"You and Rosa seem to get along well," Toby observed.

"I like her a lot. I wish we could go to school together." She glanced quickly in Chris's direction. "And it's not right that Chris and his friends tease the Catholics."

"What does your brother do?"

"They stand outside the Catholic school and yell, 'You'll burn in …,'" she lowered her voice as pronounced the letters, "'H-E-L-L.'"

Chris kicked at her sister. "Tattletale. You didn't have to tell Dad that." He looked at Toby. "Gosh, Dad. They say the same thing to us. Besides, it's sort of like a joke. When school's over, we go play ball together."

Toby spoke sternly. "That's not the way you have been raised. You need to be more considerate of other people's feelings. You can make a lot of people angry doing things like that."

Eager to change the subject, Chris said, "I heard you telling Mom that Mr. Boyd is coming back to Port Huron. When's he going to be here?"

"His uncle said he'll be back in town tomorrow. He's going to go see Michigan play Ohio State today."

Chris said, "I wish I could see a college football game someday. That would be a lot of fun."

Amanda laughed. "Who'd want to watch guys running into each other in those silly helmets and uniforms?"

Toby smiled. "About ten thousand people, I imagine. That's about how many normally attend a Michigan game." Turning to Chris, he said, "Maybe we can go next year. Would you like to play some catch after Amanda leaves?"

Amanda jumped up. "I think I'm leaving right now. I hear a car." She gave her dad a hug, picked up her book, and sprinted through the living room.

Toby watched his spirited daughter dash out the door before turning to Chris. "Would you help clean the kitchen before we go outside?"

"Sure. One thing I like about your meals is that there's not much to clean up."

When the pair was done in the kitchen, they headed to the backyard to throw a football. After a few tries, Chris threw a nearly perfect spiral. "Nice!" Toby yelled. "I think your hand is getting big enough to throw a good pass."

Chris threw another pass, and asked, "Want to see what I can do with a slingshot?"

Toby put the football down. "Sure."

"You put some cans on that tree stump, and I'll get Big Bertha."

Toby laughed to himself at the name Chris had apparently given his slingshot. When Chris returned, he demonstrated how he could hit the can from a standing position as well as from down on one knee. Toby was impressed.

"Watch this." Chris walked to one end of the yard, as far away from the target as possible. He then ran toward the target. After covering about half the distance, he fired the slingshot as he made a right angle turn. The stone hit the can, knocking it off the stump.

"Holy smokes, when did you learn to do that?" Toby asked.

Chris walked over to the stump and replaced the can. "It was something I practiced most of the summer."

"Does your Mom know how good you are?"

Chris put the slingshot in his back pocket. He looked at his dad shyly. "To be honest, Mom wasn't paying much attention to me."

They sat on the stump. Toby put his hand on his son's shoulder. "It's been a tough year for all of us."

"Do you know Mom's been doing better lately? She's not as sad anymore."

Toby raised his eyebrows. "You've noticed that?"

Chris said, "Yeah. Mom cried a lot after Natalie died. But I never saw you cry. Why?"

Toby blinked and looked away. "I thought it would make everyone feel sadder if I cried too."

"Really? When I cry, Mom tells me it's a good thing to do … that it shows how much I love Natalie. You love Natalie, don't you Dad?"

"Of course I do."

Chris said, "Gee, Dad. I wish things could the way they used to be."

Hugging Chris tightly, Toby whispered, "They will be, son. I promise."

∗   ∗   ∗   ∗

Mary sighed deeply as the train rolled to a stop at the Detroit Station. The conductor who had hovered over her since the incident at Oaks Corner, now helped her disembark from the train. He asked, "Are you sure you're going to be all right?"

Mary, weary of the conductor's constant attention, said, "Yes. My sister should be here to pick me up." Pointing to a young woman walking toward them, she said, "Here she is now."

Rebecca was about the same height as Mary, and five years younger. But her weakness for sweets made her considerably heavier. She waved as she shouted, "Mary!"

The sisters embraced warmly. "I'm so glad you were able to come. We're going to have a great day," Rebecca said happily.

"What do you have in mind?" Mary asked.

"First, we're going to have lunch here at the station. Then I'm going to take you to Hudson's and treat you to a new dress. After we do some other shopping, we'll go home for a rest. Then tonight, Frank and I are taking you out to dinner."

Mary said, "That sounds lovely."

They walked to the baggage department and asked the baggage master if he could hold Mary's suitcase until they returned.

"What time will you be back to pick it up?" he asked.

"Around three o'clock," Rebecca said.

The baggage master handed Mary a token and said, "That will be ten cents."

Mary paid the fee and turned to Rebecca. "How far is it to Hudson's?"

"Not too far. I'll drive us there, but let's eat first. I'm famished."

Once they were seated and had placed their orders, Mary asked, "How are you and Frank doing?"

"Wonderful. He just got a promotion in the accounting department at Ford. That's why we can afford to treat you for your birthday."

"You've been married two years now. Any little Franks being considered?"

Rebecca giggled as she wiped her lips lightly with her napkin. "We're really trying. Maybe it won't be too much longer."

"The two of you would make wonderful parents, and Amanda and Chris would love to have a cousin."

"I'll let you know as soon as anything happens. How are Chris and Amanda?"

"They're doing fine. Are you going to be able to come to see Amanda in her play?"

Rebecca said, "Yes. We plan on coming two weekends from now." She looked at Mary directly in the eyes. "How are you and Toby?"

Mary looked away. "Things could be better."

Rebecca took Mary's hand. "It will be, Mary. Toby loves you dearly. These things often take a long time."

Mary squeezed Rebecca's hand and smiled. "I know."

The two sisters ate quietly. When they finished, Rebecca said, "It's time to go shopping. Hudson's has the greatest new fashions for the winter season."

Within minutes they were parking the car near Hudson's Department Store. The building, constructed in 1911, was a block-long brick building on Woodward Avenue. Mary gazed up at the structure. "My, it must be ten stories high."

Rebecca said, "Yes, and they're planning to add more."

As they entered the building, Mary looked up at the thirteen-foot ceiling. "I don't come here very often, but when I do, I always get goose bumps when I first come in the door. I can't believe they can put so many things in one store."

As they arrived in the women's department, Rebecca said, "Now you look over the dresses. I need to buy some new gloves. I'll be back to see what you've picked out. Be sure to get something special. We're going to a fancy restaurant tonight."

Mary walked through row after row of dresses, amazed at how the styles had changed in the past five years. She narrowed her choices to three and went into the dressing room. Minutes later she emerged in a dinner gown of taffeta and chiffon. A large bow was fastened below the bosom. Rebecca, having returned with her gloves, snickered. "You've got to be joking! That dress is so old-fashioned; it looks like something mother would wear."

"You have any better ideas?"

Rebecca searched the racks. Finally, she held up a dress. "This is the one. It's the latest style."

Mary's eyes widened. She stared at a black satin evening gown with black lace flounces. The dress was cut low in the back and in the front. Mary laughed hysterically. "I wouldn't wear that in a million years."

They finally agreed on a blue, calf-length serge dress with a satin sash. Looking at the amount of her leg that was exposed, Mary said, "I remember that only a few years ago Toby's mother had a fit when I wore a dress that was just a few inches above my ankle."

"You look stunning. Now let's pick out some shoes and a hat to go with it."

Mary hugged Rebecca tightly. "Thanks. This has been the most fun I've had in a long time."

CHAPTER 4

▼

The wall clock read six o'clock as Russell Wilcox stood up, stretched, and looked out the front window of the modest home he shared with his mother. An autumn rain that had started about three hours prior had finally stopped. Russell turned to his mother and smiled. "I guess I don't have to walk in the rain after all."

Mrs. Wilcox continued knitting. "Are you going to tell Lillie Mae about your raise?"

"I sure am. We're going to need as much money as we can. Getting married and having children is expensive."

Mrs. Wilcox put her knitting down and looked at her son. "Has Leroy Beckwith given you and Lillie Mae any more trouble?"

Russell sat down to put on his shoes. "I think that's all over. Leroy finally realized that Lillie Mae wasn't going back to him, even if we broke up."

"I hope so. I just know that Leroy's always had a violent temper."

Russell walked over and rubbed his mother's shoulders. "Don't be worrying yourself so much. It won't do any good."

Mrs. Wilcox nodded grimly and resumed knitting. "Wear your raincoat, and don't stay out too late. I want you to take me to church tomorrow."

Russell waved as he left the house. "OK, Momma."

It had stopped raining, but the sky was full of dark, heavy clouds. Russell buttoned his raincoat as he walked down Nern Street to Lillie Mae's house. Concentrating on avoiding puddles, he did not notice a car turn off of Sixteenth Street. The car stopped, two men got out, and the car pulled away. Moments later, the car drove slowly past Russell. It stopped a second time several yards in front of him, and two men wielding baseball bats got out.

Russell stopped walking and turned around. His heart pounded faster as he realized he was being approached by four men coming from opposite directions. He ran down an alley, splashing through mud puddles. Despite the heavy shoe he had to wear on his left foot, he was able to stay ahead of the men.

Moments later, he found himself at the back fence of Stockwell's lumberyard. He pushed at a loose board and entered the company grounds. After sliding the board back in place, he hid behind a stack of lumber. Russell could hear voices outside the fence. Then all was quiet.

Russell remained hidden for nearly twenty minutes. His feet were wet and his trousers were covered with mud. He knew that Lillie Mae would be wondering where he was. Russell thought, *I can't stay here all night.* He crept slowly to the fence and removed the loose board as quietly as possible.

Russell did not see anyone as he slipped through the opening. He took a deep breath of relief and began walking. Suddenly, a figure emerged from behind a tree. Before Russell had time to react, a baseball bat smashed his right knee. Then a terrible blow was delivered to his head, knocking him to the ground. He rolled over on his back and saw the faces of four angry men glaring down at him. His final thoughts were of a herd of trampling horses as feet stomped on his face, neck, and chest.

One of the men knelt and checked Russell's pulse. "Good God, I think he's dead. What are we going to do now?"

*   *   *   *

After Russell left, Freeda Wilcox had resumed her knitting. Within thirty minutes, she found herself unusually agitated. She stood up, paced the floor, and cast furtive glances out the window. She walked into the kitchen, cut a small piece of sweet potato pie, poured a cup of coffee, and walked back to the living room.

Freeda stood in front of her corner hutch and looked at the photographs of her family. Her parents had been slaves in Mississippi, but Freeda's family was fortunate to have had an owner who was more humane than others. Slaves on the plantation were allowed to marry. Once married, a couple would not be sold separately, and none of the couple's children would be sold until they were twelve years old. Sometimes she wondered how anyone could consider any aspect of slavery humane, but Freeda knew that her parents appreciated their owner's policy.

She had been born a slave in Mississippi in 1863. Within a week of her birth, her family heard about Abraham Lincoln's Emancipation Proclamation. In a mood of exuberance, her father said that her name would be Freeda as a symbol of their newly gained freedom.

Like many former slaves, Freeda's family had great hopes in the 1860s. However, by the early 1870s, it became clear that Reconstruction was not achieving its goals. When their former owner died in 1875, the family moved from Mississippi to Chicago. Five years later they joined a small number of Negroes living in Port Huron.

Freeda looked at her own family's photograph. She had married Aaron Wilcox in 1882, and the couple had raised six children. Aaron and two of the children were deceased. Two of her children lived in Detroit, and one daughter, Patsy, was married and lived in Port Huron. Only her youngest child, Russell, still lived at home. Freeda knew that she spoiled Russell. His physical handicap had required special attention when he was a child, and Russell had been blessed with a warm, compassionate spirit.

Freeda finished her coffee and set the cup down just as a loud rap at the door broke the silence. She looked out the window and saw Lillie Mae Grant and her father. Freeda had a feeling of foreboding as she rushed to open the door. "Lillie Mae. What's wrong?"

"Is Russell here?"

"No. He left about an hour ago."

Mr. Grant put his hand on his daughter's shoulder and asked, "Did he say he was going someplace else first?"

Freeda felt her knees shaking. "No. He said he was going right to your house."

Lillie Mae cried, "Daddy, we got to look for him! Something terrible has happened!"

Mr. Grant looked at Freeda. "Do you have any kerosene lanterns?"

"I have two." Freeda ran to the kitchen to get the lanterns. "We can get some neighbors to help find Russell."

Within minutes a search party had been organized. Light from the lanterns cast long shadows as family and friends walked up and down the streets calling Russell's name.

After two hours, the search party returned to Freeda's house. Freeda's daughter Patsy took her mother in her arms. "Momma, there's nothing else we can do tonight."

Tears glistened on Freeda's cheeks. "I know, honey."

"Please stay with us tonight."

"No. I need to stay here in case he comes back."

Mother and daughter walked arm in arm. Patsy opened the door and said, "Then I'll stay here with you."

Freeda nodded. "I would like that."

CHAPTER 5

▼

Mary Sharpe followed Frank and Rebecca Wagner into the Blue Bird Club. She admired the club's elegant oak paneling, and the beautiful blue and gold ceiling. "This is lovely."

Frank Wagner smiled. "It's one of the more popular clubs in Detroit."

Mary said, "I can believe it. The place must be filled to capacity."

Rebecca said, "We were lucky to get reservations. Frank had to call a week ago to get them."

The maitre d' smiled as they approached. "Welcome to the Blue Bird Club."

Frank Wagner, a short, rotund man, gave his name. "We have a dinner reservation for seven o'clock."

The maitre d' looked at the reservation sheet. "Yes sir, Mr. Wagner. Please follow me."

Mary followed her sister and brother-in-law to the table. Once seated, the maitre d' said, "Jimmy Erickson will be your waiter tonight. I hope you enjoy your evening."

Mary noticed how similar Rebecca and her husband were physically. Both were short and rather pudgy. Both had oval faces. The shape of Frank's face was highlighted further by round glasses that had a tendency to slide down his nose.

Moments later the waiter appeared at the table. "Would you like to start with a drink? Nonalcoholic, of course."

Frank asked, "How about a grape juice?"

Mary said, "That would be fine."

Jimmy poured the juice and took their orders.

"Now for a toast to my favorite sister," Rebecca said, "Happy Birthday, Mary."

They clinked their glasses and drank to the toast. "I understand we're coming to Port Huron in a few weeks to see our niece in a play," Frank said.

"Yes. Amanda is really enjoying her experience. She likes the director and has made a new friend," Mary replied.

After additional discussion about Mary's family, Mary decided she didn't want to discuss her current marital situation so she changed the subject.

"I heard you got a promotion at Ford Motors," she said to Frank.

"Yes. I'm now supervising six accountants."

"Do you still enjoy working at Ford?"

"I like the job fine."

Mary said, "I think a lot of people were shocked last year when Henry Ford was almost elected senator. Didn't he get something like 49 percent of the vote?"

Frank nodded. "It was one of the closest senatorial races Michigan ever had."

Rebecca said, "I think people at the company were surprised he ran as a Democrat."

The waiter brought their salads. After eating for a while, Mary returned to the subject of Henry Ford. "He did present himself as the common man, so I guess it makes sense that he would run as a Democrat. And hasn't he done some good things, like raising the worker's wages to five dollars a day?"

Frank busied himself buttering a slice of bread. Mary noticed that he looked nervous. She asked, "Did my questions about Henry Ford make you uncomfortable?"

Rebecca placed her hand on Frank's. "It's OK. Mary won't tell anyone."

Frank coughed. "It's just that some of his behavior has become a little strange lately."

After the entrées were served, Frank continued. "You read about the trial in Mount Clemens last spring when he sued the *Chicago Tribune* for libel because they wrote that he was an 'ignorant anarchist,' didn't you?"

"Is that when he said 'history is more or less bunk,' or something like that?"

Rebecca laughed. "He also thought the American Revolution was fought in 1812 and that Benedict Arnold was a writer."

Mary said, "I suppose that was embarrassing, but ignorance of history doesn't mean someone is a bad person. He has written some worthwhile articles about the modern woman in his newspaper. And he has written some interesting stories about world news."

Rebecca said, "Ford doesn't write those stories. E. G. Pipp, the paper's editor, does. And Frank's heard that there won't be very many more stories like those because Pipp's going to resign."

"Why is he going to quit?" Mary asked.

Frank said, "We heard that Ford and another writer for the paper, Billy Cameron, are going to start a series of articles about Jews."

"The Jews? What is he going to write about them?"

"Ford believes that Jewish bankers caused the war in Europe."

Mary said, "Oh my. I've heard that from other people, but I didn't think Ford would put it in the *Dearborn Independent?*"

Frank sighed, "I'm afraid it's going to happen in a couple of months."

As the waiter cleared the dishes he asked, "Would anyone like some dessert?"

Rebecca asked, "Do you have any special desserts to celebrate my sister's thirtieth birthday?"

Jimmy grinned broadly. "We sure do—cherries jubilee." He walked quickly to the kitchen.

"Is it legal to serve cherries jubilee?" Mary asked. "After all, it does contain a liqueur."

Frank said, "The current law makes an exception for flavoring extracts used for cooking and culinary purposes."

Moments later, Jimmy emerged pushing a cart. He was followed by the pastry chef.

With a flourish, Jimmy stopped the cart in front of Mary. It was filled with cherries, a glass of orange juice, sugar, cornstarch, orange peels, vanilla ice cream, a cherry liqueur, and an assortment of pans and bowls. The chef mixed ingredients and heated the liqueur while Jimmy filled the bowls with ice cream. The chef carefully lit the sauce, and then spooned the flaming topping over the cherries. When the flames subsided, he poured the cherries and sauce over the ice cream. At Jimmy's signal, the band played "Happy Birthday."

Many diners joined in singing, causing Mary to blush. Then she picked up a spoon and sampled the dessert. "My goodness, this is wonderful."

After they finished eating, Frank turned to Rebecca and held her hand. "Would you like to dance?"

Rebecca looked at Mary. "Do you mind sitting alone for a few minutes?"

"Heavens no. I love to see people dance."

As Mary watched the dancers, she heard someone say, "Excuse me ma'am, but I was wondering if you would do me the honor of dancin' with me?"

Mary looked up at a handsome, smiling face of a man in his mid-thirties. The stranger had black hair parted in the middle and a small moustache. He was dressed in a three-piece blue-black worsted suit with white pinstripes. His buttoned shoes were of calfskin. Mary looked away. "No. But thanks for the invitation."

"My name is Milton Burks, and I'm just a lonely traveling salesman passin' through your lovely town. I couldn't help noticin' the birthday celebration a few minutes ago."

Mary was attracted to Milton's soft voice. She said, "Detroit's not my town. I'm visiting my sister and brother-in-law. Where are you from?"

"Southern Indiana. Were you having dinner with your sister and brother-in-law?"

"Yes. They're dancing now, but they should be back any minute."

Milton said, "If we're not goin' to dance, do you mind if I just sit and talk until they return?"

Mary hesitated, then quietly said, "I guess that's OK."

Milton chose the seat across from Mary. He smiled pleasantly. "Where're you all from, if not Detroit?"

"Port Huron. It's about two hours north of here by train."

"I see that you're married."

Mary said, "Yes, I'm married to a policeman."

"Maybe I should meet him. I'm a uniform salesman and some of my best customers are policemen. You sure I couldn't talk you into just one dance."

Mary hesitated before she murmured, "I suppose that would be all right."

Milton swiftly rose and politely held Mary's chair. He was nearly six feet tall and solidly built. Mary found that he was also an excellent dancer.

Milton said, "When are you going back to Port Huron?"

"I'm taking the eleven o'clock train tomorrow."

"Now that wouldn't by any chance be the Grand Trunk Railroad, would it?"

Mary asked, "You've heard of the Grand Trunk Railroad?"

"I'm takin' the same train to Oaks Corner. I have to deliver some uniforms."

When the song ended, Mary began to leave the dance floor, but Milton signaled the conductor and the band began playing a new Irving Berlin song, "A Pretty Girl is Like a Melody." He grasped Mary's hand and gently pulled her close, his large hand firmly placed on the small of her back. As they danced smoothly around the dance floor, Mary felt an inner warmth that had been missing for nearly a year.

When the song ended, Mary looked over at the table where Rebecca and Frank were watching. Mary said sweetly, "This has been pleasant, but I really need to be leaving."

"Of course. Perhaps we will meet again. I'll be looking for you tomorrow on the train."

Mary smiled and quickly exited the dance floor.

CHAPTER 6

▼

On Sunday morning Mary waved good-bye to her sister, boarded the train, and took a seat next to a window. She was about to begin reading when Milton Burks walked down the aisle. He smiled. "Mind if I sit here?"

Mary looked up in surprise. "Goodness gracious! I never expected to see you again."

Milton sat down. "I was wonderin' if I would be lucky enough to see you." The train jerked and then rumbled out of the Detroit depot. Milton opened a copy of *Detroit Free Press*. The two sat reading for several minutes before Milton folded his paper and laid it on his lap. "You told me last night that you were married. Do you have any children?"

"We have two. Chris is ten and Amanda is eight years old."

"I always thought two or three children would be just the right number."

"We did have three, but one died of influenza about ten months ago," Mary said softly.

Milton touched Mary gently on the knee. "I'm so sorry. How old was she when she passed?"

Mary moved her knee away from Milton. "Almost two and a half."

Milton removed his hand. "That's much too young. What did she like to do?"

"She enjoyed watching birds."

Milton asked, "Was she as lovely as you?"

Mary stirred uncomfortably in her seat. "She had dark curly hair like her father."

"I had a little sister who died when I was eight years old. It was terrible. I still think of her a lot."

Mary looked away as tears brimmed in her eyes. "It's so terrible to lose loved ones." Turning back to Milton, she asked, "Do you have any children?"

"I've never been able to find someone to marry. With my travelin', it's hard to settle down. Tell me about yours."

"Chris is interested in sports. All he wants to do is play football and baseball. Plus, he and his friends play war games a lot. Sometimes I get concerned that he might become too aggressive."

"Don't worry. Boys need to be boys. All boys need to feel like they can beat up the bad guys. What about Amanda?"

"The biggest thing for her right now is a play she's in."

"Is it a school project?"

"No. It's a community play. Most of the actors are adults, so it's an exciting, grown-up activity for her."

"Where are community plays performed in Port Huron?"

"At the Majestic Theater. They're going to be practicing every night this week because the opening show is Friday night."

"Maybe I'll just take a little trip to Port Huron and see this production when I'm done with my business."

Mary smiled, not sure exactly how to respond.

Before she said anything, the conductor yelled, "Oaks Corner, next stop."

Milton stood up and placed his newspaper on the chair. He leaned over, squeezed Mary's hand affectionately, and said, "It's been a pleasure seeing you again."

Mary nodded self-consciously. "It was nice talking to you."

Moments later, Milton was standing near the baggage car as three large boxes were removed and placed in the bed of a Model T truck. Milton turned and waved in Mary's direction.

Mary raised her right hand and was about to return the wave when she heard a familiar voice. "By thunder, it's Mary Sharpe. What are you doing on a train by yourself?"

Mary's put her hand over her mouth and gasped, "Bill." Bill Boyd had been her husband's best friend for over twenty years. He had been virtually a member of the family since Toby and Mary had moved to Port Huron seven years ago. She was especially appreciative of Bill's willingness to help find two girls who were kidnapped by Port Huron's madam, Velvet Cushion, in 1913.

Bill asked, "What's wrong? You look nervous."

"Oh, it's nothing. You just frightened me; that's all."

Mary glanced out the window to see Milton's calfskin shoes disappear into the truck.

"Is there somebody you know in that truck?"

Mary lied. "No. I was just watching them load those huge boxes."

Bill picked up the newspaper and sat down. He looked at the paper, noticing that it was open to the sports section. "When did you become interested in sports?"

Mary lied. "Oh, that's not mine. A man just threw it there when he walked by."

Bill began humming a familiar tune.

Mary asked, "Is that 'My Bonnie Lies Over the Ocean?'"

"The tune's the same, but the lyrics have been changed. Because of the unsavory behavior of some soldiers when they were in Europe during the war, the words are 'My Barney lies over the ocean, my Barney lies over the sea. My Barney lies over the ocean, the same way he lied to me.' It's a popular song on the East Coast."

Out of nowhere, Mary began laughing hysterically. At that moment she knew that whatever thoughts she had about Milton Burks, she would not allow their relationship to become a sexual encounter. She would never be able to endure the deceit.

Bill looked at Mary quizzically. "I didn't think it was that funny."

When Mary's laughter subsided, she said, "I guess I just felt in a giddy mood. Toby told me you are coming back to Port Huron to run the newspaper for a while. How is your uncle?"

"The doctor said he was doing OK. He's on a diet and exercise regimen. And he's supposed to stay away from the office for a while."

"That must be very difficult for him. I know how much he loves his job."

Bill slapped the newspaper on his legs. "It's going to be hard on the old goose. But the doctor said the heart attack was minor, and he should be able to go back to work in six to eight weeks."

"Toby told me you were going to Ann Arbor to see a football game. Did you enjoy it?"

"Are you kidding? Ohio State beat my beloved Wolverines thirteen to three. We just couldn't stop their halfback, Chick Harley. He scored both of their touchdowns."

Mary touched Bill's arm. "Well, they only got beat by ten points."

"Ten points? It might as well have been a hundred. Why did it have to be those blasted players from Ohio State? I've never seen ten thousand fans so sad in my life. But let's not talk about that wretched subject anymore. Why are you on this train this morning?"

"I visited my sister in Detroit. She wanted me to come down to celebrate my birthday."

"That's right. Your thirtieth birthday is soon, isn't it?"

Mary nodded. "I'm afraid that's true."

"Do you think we could get together tonight for another celebration? I'll treat you and your family to dinner at the Gratiot Inn. It will also give me a chance to catch up on what's been happening in Port Huron."

"Goodness, I don't know if I can handle another large meal so soon. Rebecca and Frank took me to the Blue Bird Club last night."

"Why don't we go just for dessert? I really would like to see Toby and the kids."

Mary asked, "Isn't the Gratiot Inn closed for the season?"

"The rooms are closed, but my uncle said they were going to keep the dining room open until January to see if there would be enough business between Halloween and New Year's Eve."

"OK. We'll meet you there at seven o'clock. I know everyone will want to see you."

CHAPTER 7

▼

Bill Boyd slid out of the taxi, paid the driver, and stood in front of his uncle's house. Family memories flooded his mind. His father, Abraham Boyd, made a fortune in the lumber industry in the late nineteenth century. In 1901, he founded a newspaper, the *Port Huron Star,* and handed the management responsibilities to his younger brother, Clayton.

Bill's mother died shortly after his birth, and his father died in 1903 when Bill was only fifteen. As an only child, Bill inherited a huge amount of money, becoming one of the wealthiest people in Port Huron. After his father died, Bill lived with his uncle until he enrolled at the University of Michigan in 1906. Clayton Boyd was a kind, generous bachelor who had not been much of a disciplinarian. Bill remembered the frequent teenage parties, many of which took place on Stag Island.

After graduating from college, Bill spent a year in Europe. When he returned home, he went to work for his uncle as a reporter. Bill enjoyed his job but felt the constraints of living in a small town. He had an excuse to leave when the United States declared war on Germany. Now he was back in town but wasn't sure how long he would stay. He sighed heavily, picked up his suitcases, and walked to the door.

As he approached the house, a middle-aged woman opened the door. "Mr. Boyd?"

Bill looked at the stout, unattractive woman who stood in the doorway. She was of medium height and she was thick boned. Her face was marred with smallpox scars. He nodded. "Yes, I'm Bill."

She smiled. "I'm Matilda Bryant. Your uncle hired me as a housekeeper." She moved to the side so Bill could enter the house.

Bill put the suitcases down and looked around the living room. "You certainly have managed to keep the house neater than my uncle ever did."

"Thank you. I prepared the bedroom at the top of the stairs for you. I understand it's the same one you had when you were in high school. Your uncle said you would be staying here for a while."

"That room will be fine. Where's the old sawhorse?"

"He's in his study, reading. He'll be happy to see you."

Bill always enjoyed his uncle's study. It was filled with books, mostly about history. The room also contained several filing cabinets stuffed with material on a variety of subjects that were of interest to Clayton. The files included information on everything from airplanes to the Underground Railroad.

Bill entered the study. His uncle was sitting in a high-back chair, with his feet on an ottoman. He was resplendent in a black silk smoking suit, with a red silk collar and cuffs. "Hi, boss." Bill had used this salutation ever since he started working at the newspaper.

Clayton smiled. "I hope it's OK with you if I don't stand up."

Bill walked over, and clasped the older man's hand. He looked at his uncle carefully. Clayton had lost some weight, and actually looked better than the last time Bill had seen him.

He said, "You look pretty fit."

"Dr. Nelson has me on a health regimen. I'm to watch what I eat and quit smoking. I have to start doing some exercises tomorrow. The nearest thing I have to a bad habit right now is sitting here in this fancy smoking outfit."

Bill sat down facing his uncle. "What did Dr. Nelson say about your condition?"

"He said I had a minor heart attack. It was more like a warning that I had better start taking better care of myself. And that means not working as much at the *Star*. For the time being, he said I could work about an hour a day as long as I stayed home. That's why I want you to be in charge of things at the paper."

"Is the *Star* working on anything special?"

Clayton picked up a folder from the end table beside his chair and handed it to Bill. "This is about the new automobile factory that's going to be built in Marysville."

Bill removed a brochure from the folder at looked at the first page. "Who is C. Harold Wills?"

"He started working for Henry Ford in 1902 and was one of his best engineers. In 1918, Wills urged Ford to begin producing a better quality car. When

Ford refused, Wills decided it was time to leave. Early in 1919, Wills received a 1.5-million-dollar severance bonus."

Bill continued to read. "By George, Wills is really serious. He's actually purchased over four thousand acres around Marysville?"

"Yep. He plans on building a dream city of over fifty thousand people. Read some more."

Bill read aloud. "Never before has a town in this country been designed as Marysville had. There will be ample school facilities, churches, theaters, and general amusements. There will be street car service and fast interurban cars to Detroit. Marysville will be known as the city of children."

Bill placed the brochure back into the folder. "So, Wills is going to take the little village of Marysville with its two hundred fifty people and transform it into 'dream city'? It sounds too good to be true. How far has the idea progressed?"

Clayton said, "A cornerstone for the factory is going to be laid November 15. Production of the car, which will be called the Wills Sainte Claire, is to begin late next year or early in 1921. And the town leaders are drawing up a plan to incorporate the village. They will vote on the proposal early next year."

"How much is the car going to cost?"

"Wills says it's going to be around two thousand dollars, quite a bit more than the Model T."

Bill said, "I'll say. I don't think many people will be able to afford to pay that much."

Matilda walked into the study. "Excuse me, Mr. Boyd. It's time for me to leave. Is there anything you want before I go?"

Clayton smiled. "No. If I need anything, I'll make my little scalawag of a nephew earn his keep."

Bill grumbled jokingly, "See that, Mrs. Bryant. I've only been here a few minutes, and he's already picking on me."

Matilda said, "From what I've heard, you give as good as you get." Turning to Clayton, she said, "Don't forget. Edna will be over to cook your supper tonight."

"I won't. See you tomorrow."

When Matilda left the room, Bill said, "Do you think you could have hired a less attractive woman?"

"Now stop that kind of talk. There is a lot more to life than physical looks. She's pleasant and efficient. And don't say anything about Edna either."

Bill asked, "Who's Edna? I hope she's not Matilda's double."

"She's Matilda's niece. She just moved here from Indiana to stay with her aunt and uncle."

"Indiana. Now there's a state that could have used some help naming cities. Did you know that North Vernon is in the southern part of the state, South Bend is in the north, and French Lick isn't nearly as much fun as it sounds?"

Clayton laughed. "Now that's what I mean. The poor girl isn't even here yet, and you're making fun of where she comes from. Just behave yourself when she's here."

"I'm afraid I'll miss her tonight. I'm going to the Gratiot Inn for dinner, and then I'm going to meet the Sharpes for dessert."

Clayton frowned. "The Sharpes have had a bad time of it. I hope things are better for them next year."

Bill said, "I saw Mary this morning on the train. She had been in Detroit visiting her sister. She seemed a little more nervous than usual."

"I've been told that she has been pretty depressed since the death of her child, and I hear that Toby's drinking a little too much."

"Maybe I'll be able to cheer them up tonight."

Bill jumped when the telephone began ringing. "Holy Toledo; that's loud!"

"I want to be sure I can hear it no matter what room I'm in."

Bill removed the receiver from the wall mounted telephone box. "Hello."

"May I speak to Mr. Boyd? My name is Oscar Danbridge."

"I'm Bill Boyd. How can I help you?"

"Are you the owner of the newspaper?"

"That's my uncle, but I'll be managing the paper for a while."

Oscar said, "I'm concerned about a neighbor of mine who is missing, and I was wondering if the paper could help find him."

"Shouldn't you call the police?"

"I did, but they said it was too early for them to do anything."

Bill grabbed a notebook. "OK. Who's missing?"

"His name is Russell Wilcox. He's twenty years old. He left his house last night to visit his girlfriend, and no one has seen him since."

"Can you describe him?"

Oscar said, "He's medium height and weight, a Negro, and wears a shoe with a one-inch sole on the left foot."

"OK. I'll talk to friends at the police station tomorrow. If they aren't able to help, I'll put something in the paper Tuesday."

After Bill replaced the receiver, he turned to his uncle. "A young Negro man has apparently disappeared. Let's hope they find him unharmed."

Clayton whispered, "Dear Lord. With all the violence against colored folks in other cities, that poor family must be worried sick. I read a government report a couple of weeks ago that estimated there have been nearly seventy lynchings in the United States this year. Those lynch mobs I've read about are enough to turn your stomach."

Bill said, "I'll ask Toby if he's heard anything when I see him tonight."

"If you're just meeting the Sharpes for dessert, why don't you have dinner here?"

"I've been looking forward to a meal at the Gratiot Inn. I'll start eating your Indiana food tomorrow."

Clayton frowned, picked up his book, and resumed reading.

CHAPTER 8

▼

Bill regretted his decision to have dinner at the Gratiot Inn. He knew his uncle was disappointed that he hadn't stayed home to eat. During the years they lived together, Bill and his uncle had spent their time largely independent of each other. Clayton spent most of his time at the newspaper or doing research projects when at home. Bill seldom thought about including his uncle in any of his activities. But now, things were probably going to be different. *By Jove, I'm thirty-one years old. I ought to consider my uncle's feelings more.*

He paid his bill and looked out one of the arched windows of the dining room. The eastern side of the inn provided diners with a spectacular view of Lake Huron. Bill gazed at a row of lounge chairs and made a mental note that this would probably be the last weekend the chairs would be available until next spring.

Remembering how much he enjoyed walking along the Lake Huron shore, Bill decided to take a brief stroll before the Sharpes arrived. Once outside, he noticed that the temperature had dropped considerably. He buttoned his jacket and thought, *I hope we don't have to start dealing with snow until after Thanksgiving.* He strolled along the shore for a few minutes before turning to look at the Gratiot Inn. When the Inn opened in 1916, it was an immediate hit. Its mission-style architecture, with numerous curved arches was compelling. The elegant wicker-and-cane furnishings appealed to most people. In the few short years of its existence, the Gratiot Inn had become a favorite among the "gentry-at-leisure" class. Many of the inn's summer visitors traveled from Georgia and other southern states, exchanging their hot, muggy climates for a few weeks of cool Lake Huron breezes.

As Bill headed back to the Inn, he spotted the Sharpes parking their car. He waved and walked quickly toward them. Except for a brief furlough, he had not seen the family for twenty months. He was surprised at how much older the children appeared. Chris was nearly as tall as his mother.

Amanda yelled, "Look! It's Big Bill!" She ran over and gave Bill a hug.

Bill said, "As tall as you and your brother are getting, I don't think the title 'Big Bill' will be appropriate much longer." He shook hands with Toby. "How are you doing, old chap?"

Toby smiled. "As good as could be expected. How did you like living in Philadelphia?"

"It was an enjoyable experience. I hated to leave." Bill turned to the rest of the family. "Have you all decided on what kind of dessert you want?"

Chris patted his stomach. "Chocolate cake and vanilla ice cream."

Bill led the family into the dining room. "That sounds like a great choice."

As they entered the inn, Amanda said, "It's as beautiful inside as it is outside. Look at the fancy chandeliers. Is that real linen on the tables?"

Bill said, "That's real linen. Haven't you been inside before?"

Toby said, "It's not the kind of place a family can afford on a patrolman's salary."

"Aren't you about due for a promotion to sergeant?"

"Maybe next year. The department is going to expand because of the increased population of the city. They're even going to add a position of lieutenant."

"Do you think John Gressley will get it?"

"I hope so. He sure deserves it."

They sat down and ordered dessert. Bill asked, "There's so much I want to catch up on."

"Amanda, is it true you're going to be in a play?"

Amanda smiled. "It's not a very big part, but the director, Miss Sibella, says it's really important to the play."

"I'm sure she's right, and I will make a point of seeing it." Turning to Chris, he asked, "What's keeping you busy these days?"

Chris swallowed a huge chunk of ice cream. "Right now it's a school project. Mrs. Maxwell wants us to write a history report about Michigan. But don't know what to do."

Amanda squealed, "He could go to the library! Right, Uncle Bill?"

Bill smiled, "That's true, punkin. But my uncle might be able to help you even more. He has a lot of information about Michigan history."

Mary asked, "Is your uncle well enough to do that? I thought he was supposed to take it easy."

"His doctor said he could work a couple of hours a day as long as he stays home. And I'm sure it would do him good to have someone visit him and take an interest in one of the subjects he has in his files. How about if I tell him you'll come around after school tomorrow?"

Chris said, "I can be there about four o'clock." He turned to his dad. "Can I have some more cake?"

A few seconds later, the inn's house band, the Graziadei Orchestra began playing. Amanda said, "That music sounds beautiful. Can I dance with someone?"

Bill said, "I don't know why not. Who do you want to dance with?"

"Why not me?" Mary asked. "We can show the men how good we are. I'm sure your father and Bill have a lot of catching up to do."

Toby smiled. "That sounds like a good idea. Bill, Chris, and I can do some man talk."

Amanda giggled and took her mother's hand. "OK, but you have to be the man."

Toby watched his wife and daughter walk hand in hand toward the dance floor.

Bill said, "Toby, I have a job-related question. Have you heard anything about the disappearance of a Negro named Russell Wilcox? He didn't show up at his girlfriend's house last night, and his family and friends are worried."

"No. Today was my day off. But I can check when I go to work tomorrow."

Chris asked, "Big Bill, did you see any baseball games while you were in Philadelphia?"

"I saw both the Athletics and the Phillies. They were about the poorest excuses for major league teams I ever saw. The Phillies finished in last place in the National League, and the Athletics finished last in the American League. It was more fun was going to Atlantic City to see a Negro team called the Bacharach Giants. Some of the players, like their shortstop John Henry Lloyd, were outstanding. Connie Mack, the Athletics's manager, said Lloyd could scoop up grounders and throw to first better than any white shortstop."

"I hear there are several colored teams on the East Coast," Toby said.

"I think there were nine or ten this year, plus about an equal amount in the Midwest," Bill said.

Toby said, "I think I recently read something about the Midwestern teams forming a league."

"That's right. Rube Foster, the manager of the Chicago American Giants, is trying to get things organized for next year. It's going to be called the Negro National League."

Chris asked, "If Negro players are so good, why haven't any ever played in the major leagues?"

"Because of discrimination," Bill said. "A couple of Negroes actually did play in the major leagues, but it was way before you were born. Moses Fleet Walker and his brother, Weldy, played for the Toledo Blue Stockings of the American Association in 1884."

Chris said, "But that doesn't count. The American Association is a minor league."

"Not in the 1880s," Toby said. "At the end of the season, the best team in the American Association would play the best team in the National League."

"And let me tell you something else," Bill said. "When I saw the Phillies play Cincinnati this year, the pitcher for the Reds was a Cuban named Dolf Luque. The friend I went with claimed he saw Luque play for a Negro team in 1913 that was called the Long Branch, New Jersey Cubans. After the game we went through some old 1913 newspapers, and sure enough, there was his name."

"Now wait a minute," Toby said. "You're telling me that this Dolf Luque was considered a Negro in 1913, and a white in 1919?"

Bill chucked. "Sounds crazy, doesn't it? But we kept looking through old newspapers and found five other players—Rafael Almieda, Armando Marsans, Mike Gonzalez, Jack Calvo, and Alfredo Cabrera—who did the same thing. Like Luque, they were all from Cuba. I think it illustrates one of the goofy aspects of race."

Chris asked, "What do you mean?"

Bill took out a pen and drew a line on a sheet of paper. "Let's say you define race as the color of a person's skin." He made a number of marks on the paper. "You line up every American on this line with the darkest-skinned person at one end and the lightest-skinned person at the other end, then place everyone else according to the shade of their skin." Bill asked, "How dark does this person need to be to be considered Negro?"

Toby laughed. "Are you saying there's a gray area somewhere along the line?"

"Precisely. I have a hunch these players have skin tones and other physical characteristics that allowed them to play in the so-called all-white major leagues as well as on Negro teams."

Chris sighed, "Gee, this is pretty darn complicated."

Toby looked at his watch. "Whew, look at the time. We better be heading home. You kids have school tomorrow."

Chris spoke rapidly, his words tumbling over each other, "Dad, why don't you ask Mom for a dance? I know she would like that. I would too."

Bill noticed the agitated expression on Chris' face. He scribbled a note on the paper he had been using and handed it to Toby. "Chris is right. You give this to maestro Graziadei; then go out there and dance with the birthday girl."

Toby said, "Well, I guess I'm outvoted." He stood up, walked over to the orchestra, and handed the conductor the note. Moments later, he held Mary in his arms as the orchestra played "A Pretty Girl is Like a Melody."

CHAPTER 9

▼

Homer Smoots's farm was located two miles north of Oaks Corner. A one-hundred-yard lane led to the house and a full compliment of farm buildings, including a freshly painted red barn with recently installed electric milking machines, a corn crib, and a two-seater outhouse.

Homer and two friends, Reverend Bobby Maddox and Buck Taylor, sat at the kitchen table carefully counting money and order forms. The silence was broken by Buck's annoying habit of clicking his tongue against the roof of his mouth as he counted. Reverend Maddox had glared at him several times, but Buck did not pay any attention.

The three men had agreed to organize a chapter of the Whitecaps of America. None of them had heard of the Whitecaps until three months ago. Homer was leaving a meeting at the Wolverine Lodge when a stranger introduced himself as Milton Burks. Before Homer knew it, they were talking about a patriotic organization called the Whitecaps of America. Burks told him that Whitecaps were true-blue Americans. In order to be a member, one had to be a native-born American citizen, white, and Protestant.

Burks had given Homer a pamphlet explaining the Whitecaps philosophy. The Whitecaps of America upheld the U.S. Constitution, promised to protect American womanhood, endorsed a law restricting immigrants, and supported white Christian supremacy. The group was opposed to unions, Communism, Socialism, Catholics, Jews, foreigners, and colored people.

When Homer had suggested that the Whitecaps sounded a lot like the Ku Klux Klan, Burks agreed. But he added that his organization was not as rigidly structured and was not as inclined to be violent. The pamphlet showed that the organization's home office was in Evansville, Indiana. The president was Richard Jones. The only other officer was Vice President Milton Burks. According to Burks, all the other officers would be local.

An initial year's membership came at a cost of ten dollars and included a Whitecaps uniform. Burks promised to deliver the uniforms himself if Homer could guarantee a minimum of two hundred orders. Homer went to Reverend Maddox, who in turn encouraged the congregation of the Church of Zealous Righteousness to join. When Burks called to see how things were going, Homer confidently placed an order for three hundred uniforms. Burks, pleased with the information, said that their group would be designated as District 187. As a group they could choose three people to serve as district officers. The officers were Homer Smoots, district commander; Reverend Maddox, district chaplain; and Buck Taylor, district sergeant-at-arms.

The three men had different motivations for joining the Whitecaps. For Homer Smoots, joining was primarily a political move. He was happy when Attorney General A. Mitchell Palmer established the Radical Division of the Justice Department to investigate the "Red Menace." By the summer of 1919, J. Edgar Hoover, the twenty-four-year-old director of the Radical Division, had a file containing over two hundred thousand names of suspected subversives. If the Whitecaps could help identify more subversives, Smoots would support the group 100 percent. Smoots was even considering running for state legislature in 1920 in order to promote the patriotic cause in Michigan.

The Whitecaps philosophy appealed to Reverend Maddox for religious reasons. He had become increasingly concerned about the large number of Catholics and Jews who had immigrated to the United States over the past forty years. He had read excerpts from *Protocols of the Learned Elders of Zion*. Maddox believed it to be the official minutes of a secret meeting of Jews in Basel, Switzerland, in 1897. The *Protocols* told how Jews were going to undermine Christian governments around the world. Ominously, a recent publication of the *Protocols* displayed a cover showing the symbol of the anti-Christ—a cross with three lines, two horizontal and one at a forty-five degree angle—beside the Jewish star.

Even more threatening to Reverend Maddox was the Catholic Church. He believed that the Roman Catholic Church intended to overthrow the U.S. government and move the Vatican to Indiana. He was also convinced that the Knights of Columbus donated a rifle to the Catholic Church every time a Catholic child was born, and that the sewers at Notre Dame University were filled with guns. He went to bed each night agonizing on what he believed to be the inevitable war between Catholics and Protestants.

Buck Taylor's concerns were racial. He did not believe that Negroes were equal to whites, and he felt Negroes did not deserve the same rights as whites. He had never personally known a Negro, so he had no firsthand knowledge of how they behaved. What little Negro behavior he had observed in visits to Detroit reinforced the preconceived prejudices he had learned from his parents. He was also influenced by movies, particularity *The Birth of a Nation*. Buck was greatly impressed by the film's portrayal of Negroes as subhuman brutes and the Ku Klux Klan as heroic. He was already a member of the KKK, but he joined the Whitecaps because he was given an opportunity to be an officer.

Homer Smoots stood up and walked to the stove to pour a cup of coffee. He was a large man. Dressed in an undershirt and bib overalls, he displayed the distinctive skin tones of someone who had spent a lifetime working in the sun wearing a long-sleeve shirt and a straw hat. His neck, hands, and forearms were tanned deeply, while his muscular biceps and forehead were as white as snow. He returned to the table and sat down. "Looks like everything balances. We got two hundred and ninety-two orders at ten dollars each, which matches the two thousand nine hundred and twenty dollars we have in cash."

Reverend Maddox asked, "What about the eight extra uniforms?"

Homer put eighty dollars on the table. "I'll pay for them. Maybe some people will show up Friday who didn't send in an order."

Buck mumbled, "Ten dollars sure is a lot of money for a uniform. That's more a day's wages for a lot of people."

Homer's voice swelled with pride. "It may seem like a lot, but it is a small price to pay to protect our country's values. I am proud we were able to find so many patriots." He paused for a moment before continuing. "We need to put in fifteen dollars for our uniforms."

As the three men dug in their pockets for their money, Buck asked, "Why do we have to pay extra?"

"Because we get fancier uniforms. Ours are made of some kind of shiny material and the others are cotton," Homer said.

Reverend Maddox said, "We also get some money back. Exactly how much are we going to get?"

Homer looked at the contract. "It says the commander receives seventy-five cents, the chaplain gets fifty cents, and the sergeant-at-arms gets twenty-five cents for each membership sold. That means I'll get two hundred and twenty-five dollars, you'll get one hundred and fifty dollars," he said to the reverend, "and Buck gets seventy-five bucks."

Buck whistled. "Ain't that somethin'. That's more than two weeks pay at the grain elevator."

"Milton Burks said we'll probably make twice that much next year after we recruit more members," Homer told the others. "Let's talk about Friday's ceremony. I guess you both saw the thirty-foot log near the road. I cut down an oak tree, and put it in that field after I picked the corn. I'll tie a long limb on it to make a cross, and we'll put it up Friday morning."

"It sounds impressive," said Reverend Maddox. "What about the program that night?"

Homer said, "I thought I'd give a little welcome speech, then you could deliver a sermon. After that, we set the cross on fire and have everyone sing "The Old Rugged Cross.""

"Can I set the cross on fire?" Buck asked.

"Sure. I guess that would be a fitting job for the sergeant-at-arms. Just be careful because the rags wrapped around the tree will be soaked with kerosene." Homer stood up and stretched. "I guess it's time to go to bed so we'll all be fresh when we meet Burks tomorrow. It's good both of you can stay here tonight so we can be there on time tomorrow morning."

Buck asked, "What's goin' to happen besides givin' him all this money?"

"He said he had a little swearing-in ceremony for the officers."

The three men went to bed. As they slept, visions of union workers and Communists, Catholics and Jews, and black men with white women danced in their heads.

CHAPTER 10

▼

On a beautiful Monday morning Sylvia Pointe walked eagerly down Military Street toward the Woman's Benefit Association building. Bicycling and walking helped her maintain an attractive figure. She had beautiful brown eyes and sandy-colored hair that she wore in a short bob.

Sylvia, in her early forties, had worked for the Port Huron police station for nearly twenty years. When the Great War started, she quit her job and joined the Red Cross Motor Corps. She was assigned to Camp Custer, located six miles west of Battle Creek, Michigan.

Camp Custer was built in 1917 to train soldiers from Michigan. In the government's haste to build the camp, no one thought to provide adequate transportation. There were no trains, streetcars, or busses running directly to the camp. The Red Cross Motor Corps provided the vital service to meeting recruits in Battle Creek and transporting them to Camp Custer.

When the war ended, Sylvia decided not to return to her job at the police department. She found a job at the Woman's Benefit Association as Director of Social Programs. She was excited about her new job, which allowed her to travel throughout Michigan promoting the financial and social philosophy of the WBA. She was about to embark on a five-day trip throughout southern Michigan encouraging women to register to vote.

Sylvia had another reason for enjoying her new job. The city regulations prohibited her from marrying someone in the same department. Now that she was employed at WBA, she and Detective John Gressley would be able to marry.

Sylvia stood on the steps and looked at the building. It was constructed of light gray Indiana limestone. The building was reminiscent of the Renaissance, with Corinthian columns in the front. She entered and immediately noticed the lobby floor's cream-colored marble with green veins. What impressed Sylvia the most was the stairway. It seemed like something from a Rockefeller mansion. The stairway was wide and turned to both the right and left when it reached the second floor. She fantasized having her wedding in the lobby. She and her bridesmaids would descend the stairs with a regal air. Her other fantasy was that she would slide down the banister into John Gressley's arms. He would stand there holding her, with a bemused look on his handsome face. Then Bill Boyd, who seemed to never have a thought he was capable of suppressing, would say, "I thought the idea was to catch the bride's bouquet, not the bride."

Sylvia shook her head. *Forget about your wedding plans for now. It's time to focus on why I'm here today.* She knocked on Bina West's door. Bina had been the driving force of the Woman's Benefit Association for years. She was a teacher when she became a member of the association's Capac, Michigan, chapter in 1891. Soon she was working for the organization. In 1911, she was appointed supreme commander. Bina was also active in women's issues. In 1908, she was one of America's delegates to the International Council of Women in Geneva, Switzerland.

Now, fifty-two years old, Bina was full figured and had a round face and inquisitive eyes. She smiled when she saw Sylvia at the door. "Good morning, Sylvia. Come on in."

Sylvia entered the office and sat down. "Thank you for seeing me this morning."

"This is a very important trip, so it's good we are able to talk about it some more before you leave. Do you have your itinerary?"

"I'm taking the Grand Trunk Railroad to Lapeer today. I continue on the railroad to Flint tomorrow, take the interurban to Rochester Wednesday, then I'm back on the Grand Trunk to go to Oaks Corner on Thursday. I plan to stay in Oaks Corner Friday night before returning to Port Huron on Saturday."

"That's fine. I hope you like to travel, because you will be making several of these trips. We want to make sure as many women as possible are ready to vote in the national election next year."

"I'm looking forward to it. I enjoy traveling, and the message is an important one to me. At each of the four stops I'll spend the evening talking to women about why it's necessary that they vote and how they go about registering. Then I'll talk to the local WBA officers in more detail the following morning."

"I'm sure you'll do a great job. Do you have any questions?"

"I can understand why I'm going to Lapeer, Flint, and Rochester. But why Oaks Corner? It seems so small."

"This is an attempt to provide a service to the rural women in southern St. Clair County and northern Macomb County." Bina opened her engagement book. "I would like to see you a week from today at ten o'clock. You can give me a report on how things went."

Sylvia wrote down the time. "I'll give you a full accounting." She stood up and shook Bina's hand.

Outside, she began whistling George Gershwin's popular tune, "Swanee." As she got into her car to drive to the railroad depot, she thought, *Maybe I won't tell her everything.* The reason she was staying the extra night in Oaks Corner was because John Gressley was going to meet her there.

CHAPTER 11

▼

Irene Stockwell smiled as Mr. Bannister walked into the office of the lumberyard. She asked, "Did you finish your rabbit hutches?"

"Yes, indeed. Now I decided to build some shelves in my garage. I need a couple of two-by-eights, braces, and nails."

"The two-by-eights are out by the lean-to. You pick what you want, and I'll have one of the men help you carry it to your wagon. Just be careful of Tiger. He likes to be in that area."

Bannister said, "Tiger's one of the wildest cats I've ever seen."

"True, but he's also the best mouser we've had in years."

"Do you think that colored boy could help me? He really knows what he's doing."

Irene looked down at her hands. "He hasn't shown up yet, but as soon as he does, I'll send him out. I'll get the braces and nails while you pick out your wood."

When Bannister left the office, Irene cast a worried look at her husband. In the five years that Russell had worked for them, he had never been late.

The lean-to was located along the lumberyard's western property line. The inclined roof ranged from twenty feet high in the back to ten feet in front. A number of two-by-fours held the roof and walls in place.

Bannister found the stack of two-by-eights and was examining the wood when he heard a cat hiss. He looked up to see Tiger glaring at him. The cat's back was arched, and his sharp teeth were bared. It appeared as though the cat was protecting something. He said, "You can stop that hissing anytime. I'm not going to bother you."

Then he saw what the cat was protecting Russell's bruised and bloodied body hung from a rafter of the lean-to. Bannister's eyelids twitched, as though his brain refused to acknowledge what he saw. When the frightening sight finally registered, he managed to whisper, "Jumping Jehovah," before he vomited. Not bothering to wipe the regurgitated breakfast from his shoes, Bannister quickly ran back to the office.

*   *   *   *

After the cat had been lured away, Russell Wilcox's body was carefully lowered. His face had been beaten so severely, it was impossible to recognize him. But Russell's distinctive left shoe enabled the owner of the lumberyard to easily identify him.

Detective John Gressley stood quietly as the coroner examined the body. Nearly fifty years old, Gressley was tall, with gray hair and a well-groomed moustache.

Turning to Gressley, the coroner said, "The poor boy was beaten to death. The hanging appears to have been some kind of ceremonial act."

"When was he killed?"

"Twenty four hours ago; maybe longer."

Gressley asked, "Do you have any idea what the murder weapon was?"

"Murder weapons, I'd say." The coroner pointed to the back of Russell's head. "He was hit with something like a baseball bat, but I don't think that killed him. By the looks of all the bruises on his neck and chest, I would say he was stomped to death. There were probably three or four attackers."

"Judging from the footprints, I'd agree," Gressley said.

He helped the coroner pick up the body and place it in the coroner's truck. "I sent a patrolman to notify Russell's mother. She'll be meeting you at your office later this morning," Gressley said.

Because of the heavy rain that occurred prior to the murder, Gressley was easily able to discern the footprints. He could also see how the body had been dragged to the lean-to from the fence, a distance of about forty feet.

Just as Gressley was about to take a walk to the fence, he noticed Patrolman Toby Sharpe getting out of a car the police department had rented especially for the investigation. It was 1919, and the city of Port Huron had yet to provide its police department with an automobile. Gressley thought, *Maybe someday we'll have one.* Of course, since Gressley had never learned to drive, it wouldn't be his anyway.

Gressley waved to Toby. "Did you see Mrs. Wilcox?"

Toby, carrying a fingerprint camera and a detective kit that included a regular camera, magnifying glass, and fingerprinting material, jogged over to Gressley. "Yes. She was expecting something like this, but it was really rough on her anyway. Russell's fiancé, Lillie Mae Grant, is going with her to the coroner's office."

"Did you tell her we would like to speak with them this afternoon?"

"Yes. I told them we would be there about two o'clock."

"Good. Let's start over there at the fence."

As they approached the fence, Toby noticed the loose boards. He and Gressley crawled through the fence, and Gressley pointed out an area where the ground was disturbed. "The attack must have started here. I want you to take a number of photographs of this area, particularly of the footprints."

Toby said, "Look at that one right heel print. There's some kind of odd oval marking on the right side of it."

After examining the area where the attack took place, Toby and Gressley walked slowly back to the lean-to, following the dragged body's path. Gressley picked up the rope that had been used to hang Russell. He asked, "Have you ever seen a rope like this?"

Toby shook his head. "Nope. Do you think we could get fingerprints from it?"

"I doubt it. Did you see anything that could have been used as a murder weapon?"

"No. It looks like they took all the weapons with them."

"I think you're right. Let's go back to the lumberyard office and talk to the owners."

As the two men walked, Toby asked, "Do you think the murder was premeditated?"

"Based on the locations of the footprints, I think they were waiting for him. Whether they were waiting specifically for Russell or not is hard to tell."

"Why would people do such a violent thing?"

Gressley said, "It could have been racially motivated. But we can't rule out personal reasons. Someone might have been angry or jealous of Russell."

As they approached the office, Toby began walk with added caution. He had noticed Irene Stockwell talking soothingly to a large cat near the door.

Gressley noticed Toby's behavior. "I take it you don't like cats."

Toby smiled. "I don't mind cats, but that thing is huge. Are you sure it's not a cougar?"

"Richard Stockwell said that his wife was one of two people who could get close to it. The other person was Russell Wilcox. He thinks the cat must have stood guard on the body since Sunday morning."

Gressley introduced himself and Toby to Irene. "Could you come inside? We would like to talk to you and your husband about Russell Wilcox."

Irene stood up and followed the men inside where Richard was posting a sign that the lumberyard would be closed for the day. The cat immediately ran toward the lean-to. Irene said, "The police want to ask us some questions."

"We need to learn as much about Russell Wilcox as possible," Gressley said. "I understand he has worked here for several years."

"Yes. He's been here for five years," Richard said. "He started working summers while he was still in high school. We never had any problems with him. Russell was very conscientious."

"Did he get along with the customers?"

"Some seemed uncomfortable when they first met Russell. But once they got over the fact he was colored, most of the customers liked him," Irene said.

Toby asked, "What about the other employees?"

It was Richard's turn to answer. "I think a couple of them resented the fact that some customers like Mr. Bannister would ask for Russell, but I have a hard time believing that they would do something like this."

Irene held her husband's hand. "I've heard some talk about how some thought Richard and I gave Russell special treatment."

Gressley asked, "Could you give me their names?"

Richard hesitated. Irene squeezed his hand. "It's OK. They need to know the names so they can do a thorough investigation."

"They are Boone Eckard and his buddies—Hank Peters, Lester Johnson, and Harry Moss. I tried to talk to Boone about it a couple of times, but he would just stare at me. They won't be here today because I sent everyone home."

Gressley said, "We'll be back tomorrow morning to see them." He picked up the rope that had been removed from Russell's neck. Irene gasped and put her hands over her mouth.

Gressley asked, "Do you sell rope like this?"

Richard looked at the rope carefully. He said, "No. That looks like a special kind of rope that might be used in a circus or a Wild West show."

"How can you tell?"

"See how tight the strands are? And the rope was probably bleached to get it that white."

Gressley stood up and thanked the couple for their time. "Patrolman Sharpe and I will be back tomorrow. If you think of anything that might help us, please let us know."

CHAPTER 12

────────── ▼ ──────────

The Hillside Inn, owned by Earl and Myrtle Terwiliger, was located two blocks east of the Oaks Corner railroad depot. The inn was a substantial white clapboard building with a dining room and two large bedrooms on the first floor. Five smaller bedrooms occupied the second floor. It was in one of these smaller bedrooms where Milton Burks had spent the night. Dressed in a stylish brown sack suit with a small check design, he stood in front of the mirror adjusting his tie. He then buttoned his tan vest and walked downstairs.

Myrtle Terwiliger greeted Milton as he approached the dining table. "Good morning, Mr. Burks. How did you sleep last night?"

Milton smiled sweetly. "Like a baby. The bed was very comfortable." He inhaled deeply. "That coffee smells wonderful."

Myrtle filled his cup. "Most people like our coffee. Today we're serving mushroom omelets, pan-fried potatoes, bacon, and toast."

"Great, I'm as hungry as a bear."

"You have a delightful accent, Mr. Burks. Where are you from?"

"Southern Indiana. I was hopin' time spent away from my hometown would alter my accent, but I guess not."

Earl Terwiliger entered the room. "Morning, Mr. Burks. I just checked on your crates in the garage. They got through the night without any problems."

"Good. Homer Smoots will pick them up at ten o'clock."

Earl looked at Milton curiously. "Those crates don't have anything to do with that racist meeting Smoots is sponsoring Friday night, do they? I don't like what he's doing one bit."

"I don't know if I agree with what he's doing either, but I'm just a humble salesman deliverin' some merchandise."

"I understand what you mean. Some of the participants are staying here Friday night. I guess if I'm going to take their money, I can't criticize you for doing the same thing."

Milton smiled. "I assure you that I will not be participatin' in their games. That's four days from now, and I will be long gone. In fact, I would like to pay my bill as soon as I'm done with breakfast as long as I can use the room until noon. I'll be takin' the one o'clock train for Detroit."

Milton finished his breakfast and paid his bill. He refilled his coffee cup, walked outside, and settled into a rocking chair on the porch. He was just finishing his coffee when Homer Smoots and two other men arrived in a horse-drawn wagon. "Nice seeing you again, Mr. Smoots," Milton said as he approached the wagon.

Homer and his friends climbed down from the wagon. "This is Reverend Bobby Maddox and Buck Taylor." Both Maddox and Taylor were short, but Taylor was muscular, while Maddox was flabby. Maddox had a toothy grin that could easily switch to a condescending sneer.

Milton shook their hands warmly. "Pleased to meet you. The uniforms are right here in the garage. We can load them onto the wagon first and then retire to my room."

Buck asked, "Did you hear about the nigger that got killed in Port Huron? He was beaten up and hanged."

Homer, his political ambitions showing, said, "Now we can't abide that kind of violence. Isn't that right, Milton?"

Milton looked at the men solemnly. "You are correct, Mr. Smoots. The Whitecaps of America organization doesn't endorse violence, except when necessary."

Buck shrugged his shoulders. "Maybe what happened in Port Huron was necessary."

After the four men loaded the crates onto the wagon, Milton led the way to his room. Prominently displayed on a small table in the middle of the room was a Bible, a copy of the United States Constitution, and several pamphlets about the Whitecaps of America. Pointing to the couch and two chairs, Milton said, "You all make yourselves comfortable."

Once the men were seated, Milton opened his suitcase and withdrew several garments that resembled graduation gowns. The cotton gown he spread on the bed was white with a black hem around the bottom. He said, "This is the regular uniform that I showed Mr. Smoots a couple of months ago. There are three hundred more just like it in the crates." He held up a hood that resembled a chauffeur's cap with a mask attached. "Each person will also get one of these caps."

Homer opened a box and withdrew stacks of money. "At ten dollars a piece, that comes to three thousand dollars."

"That's right," Milton said as he displayed another garment. "These are the special uniforms for the officers. They're fifteen dollars each, so the total bill comes to three thousand and forty-five dollars."

Homer handed the money to Milton. After verifying that the amount was correct, Milton handed Homer two hundred and twenty-five, the reverend one hundred and fifty, and Buck seventy-five dollars—their commission. He said, "You should be proud of the number of people you recruited."

Milton stood up. "In order to officially recognize your group as Whitecap District Number 187, I would like for you to participate in a little ceremony. First, we need to slip into our uniforms."

As Reverend Maddox dressed, he asked, "What's District Number 187 mean?"

"That's how many Whitecap groups there are," Milton replied. "And each one averages about four hundred members, so that means there are about seventy-five thousand members total. We hope to double that number next year."

When the men finished putting on their uniforms, Milton said, "Now that you're all dressed, it's time for a swearing-in ceremony." The three men looked at Milton and each other with a mixture of self-consciousness and pride. Milton wore white; Homer was attired in pale blue; the reverend wore red, and Buck donned a black robe. Milton said, "Your colors stand for district commander, district chaplain, and district sergeant-at-arms."

Milton handed each man a Whitecap pamphlet. "I want each of you to raise your right hand and read the Whitecaps of America creed."

Lead by the reverend, the men read, "We swear to uphold the Bible and the United States Constitution. We promise to protect American womanhood, endorse a law restricting immigrants, and support Christian supremacy. We are opposed to labor unions, Communism, Socialism, Catholics, Jews, foreigners, and colored people."

Milton raised his hands above his head. "By the powers vested in me by the central headquarters, I hereby declare District Number187 officially organized." He shook each man's hand firmly. "Congratulations. I know you'll make the Whitecaps of America proud. I'll tell President Richard Jones how worthy you are."

As they were leaving, Homer asked, "What if we have any questions? Do we write this Van Buren Street address in Evansville, Indiana?"

"Yes. But don't send any letters until the first of the year. The office is so overwhelmed with work that they wouldn't be able to answer until after the holidays."

Buck asked, "Are you going to attend our meeting Friday night?"

"No. As much as I'd like to, I have other business to attend to. I'll be leaving for Detroit today on the one o'clock train."

$$* \quad * \quad * \quad *$$

Graham Hastings stood at his room's window and watched the three men leave Hillside Inn. Buck Taylor walked toward the grain elevator. Homer Smoots and Reverend Bobby Maddox climbed up on the wagon. As the wagon began to move, Graham removed his robe. He whispered, "P. T. Barnum was right about a sucker being born every minute, and there goes three minutes worth."

Graham Hastings was a con man from Chicago. For the past two years he had been using the name Milton Burks as he sold memberships and uniforms to a nonexistent organization. Whitecaps of America had actually existed in southern Indiana in the late nineteenth century, but the group was no longer around. As a child, Graham learned about the group when he and his family vacationed in the resort town of French Lick. That was when he also perfected an authentic sounding Indiana accent.

For the past two years, Graham Hastings had visited Wisconsin, Illinois, Indiana, Ohio, Pennsylvania, New York, and Michigan, claiming to organize Whitecaps districts. His net profit was close to thirty thousand dollars.

Graham slipped some of the money into a money belt. He put the rest in a false bottom in his suitcase. Although the Whitecaps had been one of his most successful scams, he knew it was time to end the ruse. The longer he continued, the more likely he would get caught. Also, the increasing popularity of the Ku Klux Klan was making it harder to find prospective members for the Whitecaps. He was thinking of becoming a legitimate businessman.

Graham looked at his watch. It was now 11:30 AM. He had deliberately misled the three men about taking the one o'clock train to Detroit. Graham remembered an incident in Milwaukee when the men he sold uniforms to tried to steal his money when he walked to the train station.

Graham would return to his wife in Chicago by the end of the week, but now it was time to contact Mary Sharpe. He made it a point to have an affair during each of his escapades. These sexual encounters didn't mean anything, because he dearly loved his wife and children. But, being a good con, he enjoyed the challenge of seducing an attractive woman like Mary Sharpe. Knowing that her husband was a policeman made the enterprise more exciting.

He smiled at his refection in the mirror as he remembered telling Mary about how sad he had been as an eight-year-old when his sister died. Telling lies convincingly had been a characteristic of his since childhood. Graham picked up his suitcase and hurried to the depot to board the twelve o'clock train for Port Huron.

CHAPTER 13

▼

Detective John Gressley and Patrolman Toby Sharpe had a hurried lunch before returning to the Port Huron police station. The secretary smiled when they entered the office. She motioned to Gressley. "Chief Chambers wants to talk to you."

Gressley nodded. "Toby, go ahead and check the files for Boone Eckard and his cronies. Take the material into my office. I should be back in a few minutes."

John Gressley began his career with the Lansing police department in 1895. A difficult divorce forced him to leave Lansing in 1903 and move to Port Huron, where he eventually became a detective, the third-ranking member of the department.

Chief George Chambers looked up when Gressley knocked on the door. Gressley entered the office and sat down. "How is the Russell Wilcox investigation going?" Chambers asked.

"The coroner said that he was beaten to death and then hanged. We talked to the owner of the lumberyard this morning. We're going to see the victim's mother at two o'clock."

"Do you have any suspects?"

"There are four employees at the lumberyard who didn't like Russell. We will be interviewing them tomorrow when they go to work."

Chambers switched gears. "The main reason I called you into my office was to give you some good news. As you know, the Port Huron city officials gave their OK for a position of lieutenant, effective January first. I'm going to put you in that slot. It will mean a 20 percent increase in pay."

"That's great. Thanks for letting me know."

"You know we wanted to do this before, but we just didn't have the money in the budget."

Gressley said, "I'm glad the city's finally going to add a sergeant and three patrolmen to the staff. We have so much more to do. The city's population has climbed from twenty thousand in 1913 to nearly thirty thousand. And trying to enforce the prohibition laws has really put a strain on the department."

Chambers said, "You're right. I don't think people understand how challenging it has been to enforce Michigan's prohibition laws in Port Huron with Canada just a few hundred yards away." Chambers tapped the desk with his fingers. "There's one more thing I want to ask. Who do you think we ought to promote to sergeant?"

"I think Tobias Sharpe is the best qualified. He's the only one on the force who took the time to master the use of the fingerprint camera. In the seven years he has been on the force, he's always tried his best. I've never heard any complaints about him."

"I hear he's been drinking a little too much lately."

Gressley said, "I'll admit that the death of his daughter has been an emotional strain on him, but I think he'll work his way out of that soon."

"Don't you think some of the other patrolmen will complain?"

"I'm sure a couple of them will be upset, but they're the types who would be angry no matter who you picked. I think it's important to choose the best qualified person."

Chambers said, "Well, I'll give it some more thought. Do me a favor; don't say anything about your promotion or the sergeant situation. I want to take a few more days before I make the announcement."

The two men stood up and shook hands. Gressley said, "Thanks for the promotion. I really appreciate it."

"I wish it could have been sooner. Now when are you going to marry Sylvia?"

"We haven't set a date yet, but I don't think it will be much longer."

Gressley walked into his own office where Toby was holding several folders and waiting for him. "Did you find anything?" Gressley asked.

"Boone Eckard and Hank Peters have been arrested a couple of times for disorderly conduct. There isn't anything on Lester Johnson or Harry Moss."

"What's the other folder?"

Toby said, "This is Russell Wilcox's file. He was arrested this summer for stealing a car, and he spent a night in jail. He was released when the car was found in Flint. Russell claimed he didn't have anything to do with stealing the car and never met the man they caught in Flint."

"Was the man from Flint a Negro?"

"Yes. So I guess it was probably a case of mistaken identity."

Gressley asked, "Was Russell ever arrested for anything else?"

"There's nothing else in the folder. And several Negroes came forward to give character references when he was arrested. They said he had never been in trouble."

Gressley looked at his watch. "Looks like it's time to visit Russell's mother."

*   *   *   *

Freeda Wilcox answered the knock at her door.

Gressley said, "I'm Detective John Gressley, and this is Patrolman Toby Sharpe. May we come in?"

As Freeda led the policemen into her living room, Gressley said, "We're sorry for your loss, and we apologize for disturbing you this afternoon. But we need to learn more about your son so we can find the people who did this terrible thing."

"I understand. I'll do anything I can to help," was Freeda's solemn reply.

Gressley asked, "When was the last time you saw Russell?"

"He left here about six o'clock Saturday night. It's only about a ten-minute walk to Lillie Mae's."

"And you never saw him again that night?"

Freeda wiped her eyes. She whispered, "No. We searched the neighborhood, but couldn't find any trace of him."

Toby asked, "How did he get along with the other workers at the lumberyard?"

"He got along OK with most of them," said Freeda. "But there is this man named Boone Eckard who was mean to Russell. Eckard and his friends would call Russell names."

Gressley asked, "Is there anyone else who harassed Russell?"

Freeda stared at the detective for several seconds.

Gressley said, "It's important that we know as much as possible."

"I suppose you'll find out sooner or later. Lillie Mae's former boyfriend, Leroy Beckwith, was angry when they broke up. When he found out Lillie Mae was dating Russell, he threatened them."

Toby asked, "When was that?"

"About a year ago. But Leroy didn't bother them once they announced their engagement."

Gressley said, "We found out that Russell was arrested last summer. Can you tell us a little more about that?"

"I don't know why the police arrested him. Russell didn't have anything thing to do with stealing that car."

Toby said, "The report stated that he didn't know the person from Flint. Is that true?"

"As far as I know, they'd never met."

Gressley asked, "Do you know of any other information that might be helpful?"

"You might want to talk to Oscar Danbridge about what happened the night before the murder. He owns Oscar's grocery store down the street. He said that a carload of whites threw a beer bottle at Russell and then started to chase him."

Gressley jotted down this information, closed his notebook, and stood up. "We don't want to take any more of your time. Please give us a call if you think of anything else."

CHAPTER 14

▼

Clayton Boyd glanced out his living room window for the third time; he was eagerly anticipating the arrival of Chris Sharpe. "Maybe he forgot to come."

Matilda Bryant smiled. "School's just got out. I'm sure he'll be here as soon as he can."

Clayton smoothed the lapel on his smoking jacket. "I suppose you're right. It's just that I've been looking forward to having someone come to the house. I guess I'll go into the study and read a little before he gets here. You be sure to bring him some hot chocolate. It looks pretty cold outside."

Moments later Chris knocked on the door. Matilda opened it and smiled broadly.

"Come on in. Mr. Boyd is waiting for you in his study."

Chris asked, "Are you sure I'm not bothering him, with him being sick and all?"

Matilda took Chris's coat. "For heaven's sake, no. He's been wanting someone to talk to all day. Now that his nephew's running the paper, he doesn't think he's needed."

Chris carried his knapsack into the study. "Hello, Mr. Boyd."

Clayton put down his book. "By Jove, you've grown. How old are you now?"

"Ten. I'm in the fifth grade this year."

"And I understand you have a challenging history assignment."

Chris said, "Yes, sir. We have to do a history report about Michigan. Big Bill told me you would be able to help me."

Clayton walked over to his desk and picked up a large folder. "I thought the Underground Railroad would be interesting. One of the reasons I saved this material was because my granddad was active in Michigan's Underground Railroad during the 1850s."

Chris removed a pencil and notebook from his knapsack. "The Underground Railroad? Do you mean the St. Clair Railroad Tunnel? That's the only underground railroad I know of."

Clayton smiled. "It sounds like that might be what I was talking about, doesn't it?"

Matilda knocked lightly on the door. "Are you two ready for refreshments? I brought hot chocolate for Chris and hot tea for Mr. Boyd."

Clayton stood up and walked over to his desk to get another folder. Turning to Chris, he asked, "Do you like hot chocolate?"

Chris looked hungrily at the steaming cup of creamy chocolate. "That sure looks good. Thanks."

Matilda placed the cups on a table near the sofa and left the room.

Clayton returned to the sofa and opened the folder. "The Underground Railroad was not underground and it was not really a railroad."

Chris looked puzzled. "Then what was it?"

"It was a term used to refer to a method of helping slaves escape from the south. The basements and attics of houses and churches were used to hide escaped slaves as they traveled. One way slaves became free was to reach Canada, and many of them came through Michigan. I don't know many of the details because it was a secret. But my grandfather told me a little about it."

"How did the runaways get to Canada?"

"There were two major routes. One came up through eastern Indiana, to Adrian, and then over to Detroit. Another route came up western Indiana to Battle Creek. Then the slaves were brought to either Detroit or St. Clair County before being transported to Canada. Some decided to stay in Michigan."

Chris asked, "Did any of them stay in St. Clair County?"

Henry and Malinda Paris came here from Terre Haute, Indiana. They were free Negroes, but that didn't prevent slave catchers from kidnapping Henry three times. The last time he was captured, it took him nearly a year to regain his freedom. They lived in St. Clair and worked as cooks at the Brown Hotel."

"Wow, that's exciting. How many slaves used Michigan's Underground Railroad?"

"Since it was secret, nobody knows for sure. But I read where at least twenty thousand came through Michigan on their way to Canada."

"Did the slave owners try to get their slaves back?"

Clayton took a sip of tea. "Oh my, yes. They paid people who were called slave catchers to try to find runaway slaves."

Did your grandfather hide slaves?"

"He was what they called a local conductor. He would help move slaves from one safe haven to another. People who hid slaves were called stationmasters. Their houses were about fifteen to twenty miles apart."

Chris asked, "Was he ever afraid?"

"I'm sure he was. One night, as he and a group traveled under the cloak of darkness, they spotted slave catchers. The group had to hide in the woods until the hunters passed. He said that he could hear every cricket chirp and every owl hoot when he was transporting runaways. He was so sensitive to sound; he swore he could almost hear the corn stalks grow."

"Gee, I guess that would be scary. Were there any stationmasters and conductors in St. Clair County?"

Clayton said, "Reverend Oren Thompson would hide slaves in his house in the city of St. Clair. Then he would row them across the St. Clair River to Canada. And there was a businessman from Marine City by the name of Eber Brock Ward who would use his ships to transport runaways across the river."

Chris began to close his notebook. "Thanks for all of the information. This will make a great report."

Clayton motioned for Chris to keep his notebook open. He asked, "Did you know that many of the Negro spirituals were used as codes for the Underground Railroad?"

"How do you mean?"

"One was called 'Follow the Drinking Gourd.' The drinking gourd was a code for the Big Dipper. If the runaway slaves followed the Big Dipper, it meant they would head north. Some of the words are, 'When the sun goes down and the first quail calls, follow the drinking gourd. For the old man is a-waitin' for to carry you to freedom, follow the drinking gourd.'"

"I never knew secret codes could be in songs. Wait till I tell my teacher! She likes us to sing. Maybe we could sing some secret code songs."

"I bet that would be a lot of fun."

Chris finished his hot chocolate. "That was really good."

"Would you like some more?"

"I would like a lot more, but I'd better get home." Chris opened his knapsack and removed a book and a slingshot so he could arrange things better.

Clayton picked up the book and read its title—*Tom Swift and his Air Scout*. "What's this about?"

"Tom's trying to invent a silent motor for airplanes. If he's successful, he's going to give the design to the U. S. government. But a spy is trying to steal the secrets. It's a neat story."

"It sounds exciting."

"Yeah," said Chris. "But it's just a make up story. It's nothing like the Underground Railroad."

Clayton pointed to the slingshot. "Does Tom Swift use one of these in the story?"

Chris laughed. "No. I just like to carry it with me. I practiced a lot this summer and got pretty good."

"Maybe you can come back another time and show me how good you are."

Matilda handed Chris his coat. As he slipped it on, Chris said, "I'd be happy to. Thanks for all the information. My teacher will be impressed."

"You're welcome. Say hello to your family."

Clayton watched Chris walk down the sidewalk. He said, "I think he got something out of our little conversation."

Matilda smiled. "I don't think he was the only one who benefited from the visit. Now how about you getting some rest before your nephew gets home from the newspaper?"

CHAPTER 15

▼

John Gressley entered his apartment and immediately sat down to remove his shoes. After rubbing his feet, he lit up a cigarette. It was his sixth cigarette of the day. He had read an article about the health risks of smoking and decided it was time to stop. But he was finding that a thirty-year habit was difficult to break.

He was about to get up to fix supper when the phone rang. He picked up the receiver.

"Hello."

Sylvia Pointe said, "Hi, John. I got a few minutes before I have to go to my meeting. How are things in Port Huron? I don't imagine there's anything new."

"Well, you would be wrong. Do you want to hear the good news first?"

"Of course."

Gressley said, "Chief Chambers called me into his office today to tell me that I will be promoted to lieutenant, effective the first of January. The job comes with a 20 percent pay increase."

"That's wonderful. It certainly took a long time, but I'm thrilled."

"He also said it was about time I made an honest woman out of you."

Sylvia laughed. "Oh, piffle. He wouldn't say that."

"He didn't say it in those words, but I'm sure that's what he meant."

"Who's going to take your place as detective?"

"They're eliminating that position, but they're going to add a second sergeant. I recommended Toby, but the chief hasn't made up his mind yet. He asked me not to say anything."

"Knowing how rumors fly in that place, how long do you think that will be a secret?" She asked rhetorically before changing the subject. "What time will you be arriving at Oaks Corner on Friday? Maybe we could have a special celebration for your promotion."

"We might have to put that on hold."

Sylvia asked, "Do you mean you're not coming? Why not?"

"I'm investigating a murder. A Negro named Russell Wilcox was beaten to death and then hanged Saturday night."

Sylvia said, "That's terrible. Where did it happen?"

"At the Stockwell lumberyard where he worked."

"Do you have any suspects?"

"We've learned that some of the employees at the lumberyard harassed him, that his girlfriend's ex-boyfriend was angry, and that a group of whites threw a beer bottle at him Friday night. Toby and I are going to start interviewing people tomorrow."

Sylvia sighed. "I hope you're able to find the killers soon." She paused for a moment, then said. "I have to run; it's time to speak to a group of women about registering to vote. We're getting a lot of good publicity here in Lapeer. I'll be at the Hillside Inn in Oaks Corner Thursday night. I'll call you to see how things are going. I love you."

"I love you too."

CHAPTER 16

▼

Bill Boyd got a firm grip on the brim of his hat and threw it at one of the pegs on the hallway coatrack. He missed. In nearly two hundred tries, he had successfully landed the hat on the peg only three times. As he bent over to retrieve his hat, Clayton appeared from the dining room. "Glad to see you home in time for supper," he said.

"Something smells great. What are we having?"

"Edna fixed roast chicken and sweet potatoes."

"Edna?"

Clayton grunted. "I told you about her yesterday. She's Matilda Bryant's niece. She comes over in the evening for a few hours. If you weren't in such a hurry to get to the Gratiot Inn, you would have met her last night."

"If she's no better looking than her aunt, I don't think I missed much."

"There's more to life than good looks. Now, since we're having chicken, I think we need a bottle of white wine. Would you get one from the basement?"

When Bill entered the basement, he let out a loud whistle. Lined up along two of the walls were wine shelves filled with bottles. *By Jove, I can see that my uncle isn't going to allow prohibition to stop him from drinking.* He selected a German piesporter and returned to the dining room.

Bill placed the bottle on the table. "That's quite a collection downstairs."

Clayton grinned. "Two hundred and forty-three bottles. I started saving a couple of years ago. I figure that if we drink one bottle a week, we should have enough to keep us going until the government comes to its senses and does away with this foolishness."

"Aren't you afraid of being arrested?"

"Not once it's in the house. According to state law, warrants can't be issued to search a private dwelling unless some part of it is used for a business. So far it's pretty easy to ship things in from Canada. I don't know how difficult it will be when the federal government gets involved next year."

Bill said, "It's strange how we legalize some drugs, but not others. It's illegal to drink alcohol, but legal to smoke marijuana. Heck, marijuana's even prescribed for various conditions—labor pains, nausea, and rheumatism."

"I'd pass a law against marijuana just because it stinks so much," Clayton added.

Bill reached for the corkscrew. "Are you allowed to drink wine?"

"The doctor says it's OK as long as I don't drink more than three or four ounces a day."

Bill looked at the place settings. "I see three plates. Is what's-her-name going to eat with us?"

"Of course. She didn't want to, but I insisted. And I don't want you making any sarcastic comments about her. She's not exactly Mary Pickford, but she's really nice."

"Then I take it she looks like her aunt."

"No. Matilda and Edna are related by marriage. Matilda is married to Edna's uncle." Clayton gave his nephew a gentle shove. "Go see if she needs any help."

Bill poured the wine, then headed toward the kitchen where he found Edna tending to something on the stove. "Hi, Edna; I'm Bill. Can I be of some assistance?"

Edna turned to face Bill. She was tall—only a few inches shorter than Bill—slim, and flat-chested. Her features were rather ordinary, with the exception of her neck which appeared to be about two inches too long. Her physical characteristics, particularly the flat chest, were not appealing to Bill.

Edna said, "Pleased to meet you." She pointed to a dish on the table. "If you would take the sweet potatoes, I can get the rest."

Once the trio was seated, Bill picked up the wine bottle. "Edna, would you like to partake of the beverage of the gods?"

Edna smiled and looked at Clayton. "You were right. He does have an interesting way of expressing himself." She held up her wine glass. "Yes, thank you."

Bill looked suspiciously at his uncle. "Have you two been talking about me?"

Clayton coughed. "Don't worry. You haven't been the focus of our conversations. Your name's just come up a few times since I found out you were going to be here for a while." After pausing for a moment, he said, "Edna's from Indiana. Her father owns a farm near North Manchester."

Bill said, "I hope it's in the northern part of the state."

Edna laughed. "Yes, unlike North Vernon, which is in the south."

"So you've heard that joke."

"Almost everybody in Indiana is familiar with it."

Bill chuckled and said, "Tell me more about yourself."

Edna finished chewing before she answered. "I graduated from high school in 1916 and went to work at the army hospital in Indianapolis during the Great War."

"Were you a nurse?"

"No. I helped the nurses. Mostly I was just trying to keep things as clean as possible."

"But she wants to become a nurse," Clayton interjected. "One of the first things she did after arriving in Port Huron this summer was to take a Red Cross class on elementary hygiene and home care. Helen Davidson was her teacher. When she saves enough money, she plans to go to nursing school."

"That's an admirable goal," Bill said. "How did your uncle wind up in Port Huron?"

"He works at Mueller Metals Company as an engineer. He was one of the first people Oscar Mueller hired when he founded his factory in Sarnia seven years ago. Uncle Jeffrey helped Mueller set up the factory when it moved to Port Huron in 1917."

Clayton added, "Mueller made quite a name for himself when his company became the first in the United States to commercially produce brass forgings used to make fuses for artillery shells during the war. Edna's uncle helped design them."

As the meal was winding down, Edna said, "Maybe I should clean the kitchen. I'm sure the two of you have things you want to talk about."

Heavens no, girl. You stay with us," Clayton said. "Bill can help you when we're done."

Bill cast a wry smile at Clayton, and thought, *As a matchmaker, my uncle's about as subtle as a sledgehammer.* He said, "I'd be more than happy to help later. Did Chris Sharpe drop by today?"

"Yes. We had a wonderful time talking about the Underground Railroad. He seems like a bright little chap. He got so enthusiastic about songs with codes; he's going to see if his teacher will let the class sing them." Clayton wiped his mouth with his napkin. "Were you able to get an update on the disappearance of Russell Wilcox?"

"I talked to Chief Chambers. Wilcox's body was found this morning. He'd been beaten to death and then hanged. Chambers said it was too early to say much more."

"Who's in charge of the murder investigation?" Clayton asked.

"John Gressley and Toby Sharpe. They were out all day, and I had to stay close to the office, so I didn't get a chance to talk to them."

Edna said, "My aunt told me the victim was colored. Do you think the attack had to do with race?"

Bill shrugged his shoulders. "It's hard to tell. There has been a lot of racial violence this year. Groups like the Ku Klux Klan certainly promote that type of thing."

"And not just against Negroes. Some of the Klan's views about Catholics are astonishing," Clayton added.

Edna giggled. The two men looked at her. Bill asked, "Why is that funny?"

Edna blushed. "I'm sorry. I just thought of an incident that happened in North Manchester. Many people in Indiana believed that the pope was going to relocate the Vatican in our state. One day, a Klan lecturer said that the pope was actually on a train and would be in North Manchester the next day. More than one thousand people were at the train station when a little bald-headed man got off the train. Someone yelled, 'That's the pope!'"

Bill asked, "The pope? They thought he would be traveling alone?"

"I guess so. The poor guy claimed he was a corset salesman. He actually had to open his suitcase to show all the corsets he had. They finally left him alone, thinking that the pope wouldn't be carrying that many corsets."

The two men burst into laugher. Bill asked, "Are you making that up? Why didn't we ever read about it in the papers?"

Edna crossed her heart. "It's the truth, honest. My older brother was there. I don't think it was ever written up because the local newspaper was too embarrassed to make public how silly the people in North Manchester had been."

Clayton stood up and stretched. "That's about enough excitement for me tonight. I think I'll go to the study. Bill can help you clean the kitchen." Clayton started to leave the dining room, but first stopped and said, "Oh, Bill, ask Edna about baseball." Concealing his right hand from Edna and Bill, Clayton crossed his fingers as he exited.

Edna and Bill cleared the table and carried the dishes to the kitchen. Bill said, "That was a delicious meal. Did your mother teach you to cook?"

"A little. But my aunt actually prepared the meal. I just followed her instructions in finishing it," Edna said as she looked at Bill. "We didn't talk much about you during dinner. Have you lived in Port Huron all your life?"

"I grew up in Port Huron and graduated from high school in 1906. Then I went to the University of Michigan where I earned a degree in history. After that, I came back here to work for my uncle. I joined the army in 1917. Because of my journalism background, I was assigned to the Committee on Public Information and stationed in Philadelphia. I just got back to Port Huron yesterday. And that, in a nutshell, is the life of Bill Boyd."

Bill grabbed a dish towel. "If you wash, I'll dry. I take it you're a baseball fan. What's your favorite team?"

Edna filled the sink with water. "Chicago White Sox. But I'm about to change teams."

"Do you think they actually threw the World Series?"

"It sure sounds that way. I really respect that sportswriter Hugh Fulleton. When he wrote that something was wrong, he made me wonder."

Bill said, "The club's owner said that he believed his players were on the level. He even offered a twenty-thousand-dollar reward for any evidence to the contrary."

"I think he just said that to get good publicity. It's too bad he didn't spend that money to pay his players properly. It's a crying shame how little some of them got this year."

"If some of the players were involved in throwing the series, who do you think they were?"

Edna said, "Some people are pointing the finger at poor old Joe Jackson. But I don't see how someone can bat .375, get more hits than anyone on either team, and still be accused of trying to lose. If I had to guess, I would pick Eddie Cicotte and Lefty Williams. Their pitching was way off."

"I don't see why people were so surprised the Reds won. They have an excellent pitching staff. A lot of baseball experts claim good pitching beats good hitting."

"That's true. The Reds had the best ERA in the majors this year. But I still think the White Sox were the better team."

Bill put the last of the clean dishes in the cupboard and tossed the dish cloth on the counter. "Would you be interested in going to the movies sometime?"

Edna smiled. "Look, I know your uncle is trying to get us together. But, you don't have to do this for your uncle."

Bill laughed. "I seldom do anything just for my uncle. I've had a fun time tonight and would like to take you to the movies. It's a pleasure to talk to a woman who is as knowledgeable about baseball as you are."

"Then I would like to go. I have Wednesday nights off."

"Great. Let's get the newspaper and see what's playing."

Bill picked up the paper. "Let's see now ... I don't think the program at the Majestic would be appropriate. A burlesque troop called Jean Bedini's Peek-a-Boo will be performing."

Edna laughed. "You're right. I think both of our uncles would be upset."

"Wow, listen to what's showing at the American. *The End of the Road* is 'an absorbing drama in which shocking scenes impress the terrible penalties paid for ignorance and recklessness in sex relations. Wives and children reap the harvest of wild oats.' They won't let anyone in who is under fourteen."

"Let's rule that one out too. But if you're trying to make me blush, it won't work. Remember, I grew up on a farm and worked in a hospital for almost two years."

Bill said, "Wait a minute. I got just the one for a couple of baseball fans. It's called *The Busher,* and stars Charles Ray and Colleen Moore. It's about a small-town player who gets to the majors and becomes a carouser."

"That sounds like fun. I liked her in *A Hoosier Romance* last year."

"OK. It's at the Maxine, and it starts at seven."

"I don't live very far from there," Edna said. She gave Bill her address.

"I'll pick you up at six thirty. Did you know Colleen Moore was born in Port Huron? Her birth name was Kathleen Morrison. I met her a couple of times when she was a little girl."

"How did she get into movies?"

"I understand a relative of hers knew the director, D. W. Griffith," Bill said. "He helped her get started to return a favor."

Edna stood up. "I've enjoyed this evening. Thanks for inviting me to the movies."

Bill helped Edna slip into her coat and walked her to the door. "It's been my pleasure. See you Wednesday night."

CHAPTER 17

▼

Toby parked the police department's rented Model T in front of Detective John Gressley's apartment. Moments later, Gressley walked to the car and slid into the passenger's seat.

"Congratulations, lieutenant."

Gressley smiled, "That secret didn't take long to get around, did it?"

Toby put the car in gear and headed south on Erie Street. "A little birdie called last night. I guess the chief hasn't made a decision on the sergeant's position yet."

"Chief Chambers said he wanted to take a few more days before he decided."

After an awkward silence, Gressley finally said, "The only thing I can say now is that he's giving you careful consideration."

"I thought he would. I just hope they don't promote Wilbur Greene."

"With all the complaints the department has received about him, I don't think you have to worry about that. Chambers knows the other patrolmen would resent having to take orders from Wilbur."

Moments later the car pulled into the Stockwell lumberyard parking lot. Gressley had called the owner to ask that Boone Eckard, Hank Peters, Lester Johnson, and Harry Moss be summoned to the office for questioning. Gressley said, "When we get inside, I want to interview each person separately. I'll talk to Eckard and Peters. You take the other two. Be sure you find out what they were doing Saturday night, and check the heels of their shoes."

Toby nodded. "Understood."

Stockwell greeted the two policemen at the door. "The employees you wanted to talk to are here, but they're not very happy about being interviewed by the police."

The four men watched sullenly as Gressley and Sharpe entered the office. Gressley calmly ignored their stares as Stockwell introduced them.

Gressley said, "I appreciate your willingness to be interviewed concerning the murder of Russell Wilcox."

Boone glared. "Are we under suspicion? Because if we are, I'm tellin' you right now, we didn't do it." The others nodded in agreement.

Gressley said, "We're not accusing anyone right now. We're just trying to learn as much as we can. I know you want to help catch the murderers."

Boone smirked and glanced at the other three. "Sure we do. What do you want to know?"

Gressley said, "We're going to talk to you individually. I'll start with Boone and Patrolman Sharpe will interview Lester." Gressley turned to Stockwell. "Is there somewhere we can go to have some privacy?"

"You can use my private office. Patrolman Sharpe can sit in that corner in the back. I'll make sure no one bothers either of you."

Gressley led Boone into the private office. Once they were seated, Gressley asked, "Where were you Saturday night between six and seven o'clock?"

"Me and the boys were playin' poker at my house."

"Who do you mean by 'the boys'?"

Boone said, "Hank, Lester, and Harry."

"You started that early?"

"Yeah. My wife fixed us an early supper. Then we played cards until midnight."

Gressley asked, "So it was just the four of you?"

"That's right. My wife took the kids over to Lester's house." He grinned. "She can't stand swearin' and smokin'."

"What time did she leave and return?"

"She left about six and came back about ten or eleven. I wasn't payin' much attention to the time."

"Can your wife confirm that you were playing cards at six?"

Boone hesitated for a minute. "Now that I think about it, she left about five thirty. The boys got there about six."

"So the four of you were alone between six and ten?"

Boone shifted his weight. "I see what you're drivin' at. But we never left the house."

Gressley smiled. "Is there any way you can prove that?"

Boone shrugged his shoulders. "No, but we didn't kill that nigger."

"Haven't you harassed him at work?"

"Yeah. But he had it comin'. He'd get too uppity for his own good from time to time."

Gressley asked, "Who won?"

"Huh? Oh, you mean at poker? I did. I won about ten dollars."

"Who was the big loser?"

Boone grinned. "I think Harry lost the most. At least he complained the loudest."

"Just one more thing. Would you lift you feet so I can look at your shoes?"

Boone picked up his feet. Gressley examined the heels but did not find the distinctive oval pattern he and Toby had found at the murder scene. Gressley said, "That will be all for now. Please tell Hank to come in."

Boone walked toward Hank. He jerked his thumb toward Stockwell's office. "The big-shot detective wants to see you now."

As soon as Hank sat down, he began nervously bouncing his right leg.

Gressley said, "Just relax. I only have a few questions to ask about Saturday night. Where you between six and seven o'clock?"

"I was at Boone's playing poker with the other guys until about midnight."

"Who won the most money?"

Hank scratched his nose. "Boone. He always wins. Harry lost the most. I pretty much broke even."

After asking a few more questions and checking Hank's shoes, Gressley stood up. "That will be all for today."

Minutes later Gressley and Sharpe were back in the parking lot. Gressley shared what he had learned about the Saturday night poker game. Toby said he was told the same thing.

Gressley said, "Their stories match, but they don't have anybody else to give them an alibi. What about the mark on the shoes?"

Toby said, "Neither of them had that oval marking on their heels. "But they had their work shoes on today. Maybe one of them wore a different pair of shoes when they played poker."

Gressley and Toby got into the car. Gressley said, "We'll check their other shoes later. Right now I want to hear what Oscar Danbridge can tell us about the people who threw the beer bottle at Russell Saturday afternoon."

CHAPTER 18

▼

Bill Boyd spent the first two hours Tuesday morning talking with the editor of the *Port Huron Star*. As acting publisher, he didn't want to get in the way, but he also felt it was necessary to learn as much as possible. He had worked at the paper as a reporter, but he'd never taken much interest in the actual publication.

Bill grabbed a cup of coffee and went to his uncle's office. As Bill began sorting through the mail, he smiled as he recalled his uncle's transparent attempt to get Edna and him together. Bill had always dated curvaceous beauties that enjoyed parties. Edna was rather plain looking, although she did have intelligent, inquisitive eyes. Also, it impressed Bill to know that she was an enthusiastic, knowledgeable baseball fan.

Toby Sharpe, his best friend since high school, had always told him that his choices in girls virtually guaranteed short-term relationships. Up to now, that had been just fine. But Bill wondered if maybe it was time to settle down. He had always admired Toby and Mary Sharpe's marriage, although he had noticed some tension between the two of them Sunday night when they had all met at the Gratiot Inn.

He wanted to spend some time with Toby, but knew their schedules would make that nearly impossible for awhile. Unfortunately, Bill needed to spend time at the newspaper, and Toby was occupied with the Russell Wilcox murder case. A new reporter was covering the story for the *Star*, but Bill wondered if he might talk to Gressley and Toby to see if he could get more information. The more he thought about it, the better the idea sounded. He would be able to combine work with a social visit.

He picked up the telephone and rang a familiar number.

"Port Huron Police Department," said an unfamiliar voice.

"May I speak to Sylvia Pointe?" Bill asked.

"I'm sorry, but she doesn't work here anymore."

Bill thought, *By Jove, that's right. She quit when she joined the Red Cross Motor Corps during the war.* He said, "My name is Bill Boyd, and I'd like to speak with either Detective Gressley or Patrolman Sharpe."

"They're not available right now. Can I take a message?"

"Yes. Tell them that I would like to have lunch with them Wednesday. I will meet them at noon at the Harrington Hotel. They can leave a message at the *Port Huron Star,* or they can call me at my uncle's house."

CHAPTER 19

▼

Oscar Danbridge was inventorying his canned-fruit section when he saw two policemen enter his store. He put down his clipboard and waited for them to approach.

Gressley asked, "Mr. Oscar Danbridge?"

"Yes."

"I'm Detective Gressley, and this is Patrolman Sharpe. We want to ask you about an incident you observed Friday night involving Russell Wilcox. We were told that a carload of white men threw a beer bottle at him."

"That's right. He was walkin' by my store on his way home from work."

"How many were in the car?"

"There were four. Two got out, and two others stayed in the car."

Gressley asked, "Can you show me where it happened?"

"Sure." Oscar led the policemen out of the grocery store and pointed to a spot about a block away. "It happened down there. The bottle smashed all over the place when it hit that tree. I went down and cleaned it up later."

Toby said, "You said two people got out of the car. What did they do?"

"The driver wanted to chase Russell, but one of the passengers got out and grabbed the driver's arm."

Gressley asked, "Could you hear what they said?"

"The passenger yelled, 'Mike, don't do this now.' It seemed like he wanted to wait until another time to attack Russell. Then Mike said, 'Aw, Luke.' They talked some more before they got back in the car. But I couldn't hear what they said."

Toby asked, "Did you recognize either one?"

"I never saw the one called Mike before, but I'm pretty sure the passenger was that war hero, Luke Laboy. He looked like the guy who had his picture in the paper for receiving the Distinguished Service Cross when he saved six of his buddies in the Argonne Forest. It's a cryin' shame that he would come home and do something like this."

Gressley nodded. "We'll be sure to talk to Luke Laboy this afternoon. Is there anything else you might know that would help us? I understand there were bad feelings between Russell and Leroy Beckwith."

"Leroy was really upset when Lille Mae broke up with him and started dating Russell. But I don't think Leroy would do anything like this. Plus, if there was more than one murderer, the way today's newspaper said, I'm sure I would have heard something if it was colored boys. There's only about five hundred Negroes livin' in Port Huron, so stories travel pretty fast."

Gressley asked, "Do you know where Leroy works? It's important that we talk to him."

Oscar remained silent.

Gressley said, "I know you don't want to get him into trouble, but to have a complete investigation we need to consider all the possibilities."

Oscar frowned. "Leroy's a janitor at Mueller's, and I don't want to see him getting fired."

"We'll wait until he's done working. We don't want to jeopardize his job."

Oscar said, "OK, but I think it's going to turn out to be a racial thing. There's so much of that going on right now. According to the NAACP, about seventy Negroes have been lynched this year. Some were soldiers who were still wearing their uniforms. Can you beat that? A fella risks his life for his country, and what happens? He gets killed by some mob when he gets home."

Gressley nodded. "We are going to treat everyone fairly in our investigation."

"Did you ever hear of the Albert Martin lynching?"

"No. Where did that happen?

"Right here in Port Huron about thirty years ago. Martin was accused for assaulting a woman and was put in jail. A mob stormed the jail, dragged him to the Seventh Street Bridge, and hanged him." Oscar continued, the tone in his voice becoming increasingly bitter. "What was really disgusting was that not one person was ever arrested for murdering him."

The three men walked back to the grocery store. Gressley said, "Mr. Danbridge, please believe me that we're going to do all we can to bring Russell Wilcox's killers to justice, regardless of their race."

"I believe I can trust you. But some of us have been talking about starting a chapter of the NAACP here in Port Huron. It looks like we're going to have to protect ourselves the best way we can." Oscar opened the door to his store. "Did you hear that Russell's funeral is tomorrow afternoon? It would be a nice gesture if some white police officer attended. It might make the colored people feel better."

Gressley said, "I'll be there. What time?"

"It's at two o'clock at the Mount Olive Baptist Church."

"Is that a new church?"

"It just started this year. I'm one of its founding members."

Toby and Gressley got back in the car and headed toward police headquarters. Gressley asked, "Did you ever hear about the lynching Oscar was talking about?"

"No, but I was only two years old in 1889, and it's the type of thing my parents wouldn't have talked about if they'd thought I was listening." Toby turned onto Seventh Street. "What's that organization with all the letters Oscar mentioned?"

"It's the National Association for the Advancement of Colored People. It was founded in 1907 to help protect the rights of Negroes."

"I suppose they need an organization like that. Do you think there are really five hundred colored people living in Port Huron?"

Gressley said, "I guess I've never really thought about it. I was thinking about how little contact I have with Negroes. None work for the police department. I don't have any Negroes as friends. When you go into a store, they're usually in the background. But it looks like there are a lot of businesses in their neighborhoods—grocery stores, barbershops, dry cleaners, funeral homes—that cater mostly to colored customers."

"There are Negroes in the public schools, but I never had much contact with them. I remember when Kathleen Wagner got her name in the paper for being the first Negro to graduate from Port Huron High School in 1907. But she was a year behind me, and I never paid much attention to her."

Toby pulled into the city's parking lot. "What about Luke Laboy? There's a name I'll never forget. He sure gave us a run for our money six years ago with all of those breaking-and-entering crimes."

Gressley agreed. "I thought he had straightened himself out. It would be a shame if one of our city's war heroes turned out to be a murderer." Gressley glanced at his watch. "It's time for lunch. Let's meet back in my office at one o'clock to see if we can track down Luke Laboy and Leroy Beckwith."

*   *   *   *

Toby returned from lunch and headed immediately to the file room. After a few minutes of searching, he closed the file in his hand triumphantly and smiled. *I knew it*, he thought. He was still grinning when he entered Gressley's office.

Gressley asked, "What happened?"

"What do you mean?"

"You look like the cat that swallowed the canary."

Toby sat down. "When I was eating lunch, I got to thinking about Leroy Beckwith. I thought his last name sounded familiar, so I checked the file on that car theft last summer. You know, the one Russell Wilcox was arrested for?"

Gressley nodded.

"Well, it turns out that the colored guy from Flint who stole the car has the same last name as Leroy Beckwith. They just might be related. Maybe Russell's murder has something to do with the car theft instead of Russell's girlfriend. What if Russell helped steal the car? Maybe the Beckwiths were angry that he was freed, while Leroy's relative was punished. Maybe they got some people from Flint to kill Russell."

"That might explain why Oscar Danbridge didn't hear anything about any local Negroes being involved. We'll check that out when we interview Leroy. First we're going to talk to Luke Laboy."

"You know where he's at?"

Gressley stood up and put on his hat. "I found out that he and his brother opened an automobile garage a couple of months of ago. The garage is down on Military Street. I also called Mueller's. Leroy's shift ends at three o'clock. We'll talk to him as soon as we're done with Luke."

*   *   *   *

When Gressley and Toby entered Laboys' Garage, they saw Luke draining oil out of a Model T. Gressley said, "Luke Laboy."

Luke looked up. He was in his early twenties, and the scar across his right cheek served as a daily reminder of how close he had come to being killed during the Great War. A bullet had grazed his face during the terrifying ordeal in the Argonne Forest.

Gressley had arrested Luke in 1913 on a number of breaking-and-entering charges. Because he was only fifteen at the time, he was only sentenced to probation. Two years later, he became the star halfback on the Port Huron High School football team. When the war began, he joined the army and won several medals for bravery, including the Distinguished Service Cross for extraordinary heroism.

Luke wiped his hands on his pants. "That's my name." He smiled when he recognized the two policemen. "Detective Gressley. It's been a long time since I've seen you."

Nodding toward a small office in the back, Gressley said, "We need to ask you some questions in private."

Luke shrugged his muscular shoulders. "Follow me."

Once they were seated in the office, Gressley continued, "We want to ask you some questions about a beer-bottle-throwing incident that took place Friday night."

"You're checking on that? Nothing serious happened."

"Suppose you let us decide how serious it was. Just tell me what happened," Gressley said.

"This guy, Mike Sweeney, came to us because his car kept stalling. He wanted it fixed because he's taking it on a trip this weekend. We worked on it and took it for a test drive Friday night."

Toby asked, "Who was in the car?"

"Mike was driving. My brother, Mark, was in the front seat. I was in the backseat with a friend of Mike's. I don't know his name."

Gressley asked, "Can you describe Mike and his friend?"

"Mike's in his mid-twenties. He's short and skinny and has light brown hair. The other guy seemed a little older, maybe about thirty. He was kind of average height and build with dark hair. He was pretty quiet."

Gressley asked, "Do you know where they live?"

"No. Mike's parents live in town, but I don't think he's staying with them."

Toby asked, "Why were you drinking and driving?"

"We weren't drinking. There were some empties in the car. When we turned down that street, Mike's friend picked one up and threw it at the colored guy. But nobody got hurt."

Gressley asked. "According to a witness, you got out of the car. Why did you do that?"

"That fool, Mike, was acting stupid. I wanted to keep us out of trouble. Mark and I just started this business, and we don't need bad publicity."

Toby flipped open a notebook. "According to our witness, you said 'Mike, don't do this now.' Were you waiting to do something later?"

Luke wore a puzzled expression. "What are you talking about?"

"The murder of Russell Wilcox," Gressley said.

"Murder? You mean that was the colored boy that was murdered?"

Toby asked, "Didn't you read about it in the paper?"

"I haven't seen a paper today. I heard a Negro got killed, but I didn't know it was the same guy. What did your witness claim I said?"

Toby reread the statement. "Mike, don't do this now."

Luke shifted his weight. "That was several days ago. I can't remember exactly what I said, but I might have said, 'Mike, don't do this.' Then I grabbed his arm and said, 'Now get back in the car.' I sure didn't mean we were going to come back later."

Gressley asked, "Where were you Saturday night between six and seven?"

"Mark and I were closing the garage."

Toby asked, "Did anyone else see you?"

Luke sighed. "No, I don't think so."

Gressley asked, "Could you lift you feet? We want to check the bottoms of your shoes."

Luke reluctantly picked his feet up off the floor and showed the detective the soles of his shoes.

Gressley said, "That's fine. Now can we talk to your brother?"

"He's in Detroit on business. He took the train this morning and won't be back until Thursday."

Gressley stood up. "That's all for now. But we'll want to talk to your brother when he gets back in town."

CHAPTER 20

━━━━━━━━━━━━ ▼ ━━━━━━━━━━━━

After spending a restful night at the Harrington Hotel, eating a late breakfast, and stopping at Walt's Barbershop for a trim and a shave, Graham Hastings hit the banks. As was his routine, he was on a mission to exchange the smaller bills he'd received in Oaks Corner for larger ones in an effort to lighten the load in his suitcase before he returned to Chicago. To avoid suspicion, he never exchanged more than two hundred dollars any one bank, and he always claimed the money was gambling winnings. Graham entered Port Huron's Federal Commercial and Savings Bank. As always, he began to observe the tellers. When possible, he liked to conduct his transaction with a female teller, using his charm and good looks to minimize suspicion. Federal Commercial was no different. He noticed a female teller stationed behind a nameplate that read "Tina," and immediately got in her line.

When it was his turn, he walked to the teller's window. "Mornin', Miss Tina. You are certainly blessed with a lovely name."

Tina looked at Graham's handsome face, and smiled. "Good morning, sir. May I help you?"

Graham leaned close to the window. He said softly, "My, if didn't know better, I would think you are using those pretty blue eyes to flirt with me."

Tina blushed. "That's not true. I was just being polite."

"I do believe I've embarrassed you," Graham said.

Before Tina could reply he withdrew a number of bills from his inside jacket pocket. "I would like to exchange these smaller bills for hundreds."

Tina looked at the bills, and then glanced quickly at Graham.

Graham flashed a beguiling smile. "I got lucky last night rolling dice. I just want fewer bills to carry around."

Tina turned her face slightly to avoid the seductive look in Graham's eyes. She counted the money Graham had given her. "You have exactly two hundred dollars. Here are two one-hundred-dollar bills."

"Thank you very much, my dear Tina."

Graham exited the bank, convinced he had made a wonderful impression. He looked at his pocket watch. It was a little after one o'clock, but because of the late breakfast he was not hungry. He decided to go to the Majestic Theater and see what time the community actors were going to rehearse. Then he would call Mary Sharpe and negotiate a time they could get together.

As he walked down Huron Avenue, he noticed a display of shirts at Springer and Rose.

He entered the store. Pete Richmond, a young clerk with a large nose looked up. He had been a skinny teenager with a huge nose that subjected him to frequent teasing. His nose was still large, but the rest of his body had grown considerably. Consequently, he was no longer subjected to humorous comments. He smiled. "May I help you?"

"I believe you can. I would like a shirt like the ones displayed in the window."

"They're right over here."

Graham searched though the pile. He held up a blue cotton shirt with white cuffs and collar. "May I try this one on?"

"The fitting rooms are there in the back."

Minutes later, Graham returned. "It fits perfectly."

As he was paying for the shirt, he asked, "Do you know if anyone would be at the Majestic Theater this time of day?"

"Brenda should be there by now. She opens the box office at one o'clock. You can use our back door if you want. It would be closer."

Graham exited the clothing store and walked to the theater. He entered the theater, noticing that Jean Bedini's Peek-a-Boo burlesque troupe would be performing Wednesday night.

Graham approached the woman behind the ticket window and smiled broadly. "Do I have the privilege of meeting the lovely Brenda?"

Brenda appeared startled. "How do you know my name?"

"I just asked someone to tell me who had the prettiest brown eyes in Port Huron. Yours was the only name mentioned." Graham placed his hands on the ticket booth. "I didn't realize Port Huron had such a grand theater."

Brenda blushed. "It holds fifteen hundred people. We're very proud of it." She looked at Graham's well-manicured fingernails. "Do you want to buy a ticket?"

Graham grinned. "For what show?"

Brenda pointed shyly to the poster for the burlesque show. "For that?"

Graham laughed. "Oh, no. I have no desire to see scantily-clad women parading on a stage. I'm here to find out what time the community actors are rehearsing tonight. I have a good friend who is in the play. I promised to come to see him tonight, because I'll be leaving town tomorrow."

Brenda looked at the schedule. "They'll be here from six to eight. They start early because some of the cast members are children."

Graham gave Brenda a seductive wink. "Thanks. I hope I see you again, perhaps in a more intimate environment." He exited the theater, confident he had made another great impression.

He walked back to the Harrington Hotel, and stopped in the lobby to use the phone to call Mary Sharpe's home.

Mary answered.

"Hello, Mary. This is Milton Burks. Are you able to talk now?"

Mary did not answer.

Graham laughed. "Surely you haven't forgotten me already. I'll remember our dance at the Blue Bird Club forever."

Mary spoke quietly. "Yes, I know who you are."

"Well, I came to Port Huron the way I promised. I would like to see you tonight."

"I'm afraid that's not possible. I have to take my daughter to play practice."

"I know about that. She's going to be there for two hours. You could drop her off, meet me at the Harrington Hotel, and be back by the time rehearsal is over."

"My son and husband will be there too."

Graham began to get annoyed. This was not going the way he had imagined. "You can tell them you have some errands to do."

Mary paused. "I'm sorry if you got the wrong impression in Detroit, but I won't be meeting you tonight. Please don't call me again." She hung up before he had a chance to respond.

Graham stood looking at the receiver for a few moments. This was not the response he was expecting. He slammed the receiver onto its cradle. The desk clerk watched curiously as Graham stomped angrily into the hotel bar.

Graham ordered lunch and sat stewing. He could not understand what had gone wrong. As far as Graham was concerned, he had every right to believe that Mary had succumbed to his charm. However, like most con men, it did not take long for him to regain his confidence. He would still attend the rehearsal at the Majestic Theater.

CHAPTER 21

▼

Toby parked the car a block from Mueller Metals and waited for Leroy Beckwith who was scheduled to leave the factory in fifteen minutes. Toby turned off the motor and asked Gressley, "Are you still planning to go to Russell Wilcox's funeral tomorrow?"

"Yes, I think it's important that I be there."

"Why?"

"There are a couple of good reasons. One is to show the family that the police department is concerned about Russell's death. Often times Negroes feel as though crimes against them are not taken seriously. I also want to decrease the chances of a race riot."

"Do you think we could actually have a race riot in Port Huron?"

"It's a possibility we need to consider. There have been more than twenty race riots in the United States this year. Some have been in small towns, others in large cities. In some cases the riot occurred because the police did not take proper precautions."

"You mean like in Chicago when that colored boy drowned after getting hit by a rock while swimming in an area whites claimed as their beach?"

Gressley said, "That's a good example. The police refused to arrest the white man who threw the rock. Instead, they arrested a Negro who was angry because the police wouldn't arrest the rock thrower. Whites were angry because the coloreds were using a so-called white beach, and the Negroes were angry because the police didn't arrest the white man. You add to that all kinds of absurd rumors, and soon you got a powder keg ready to go off."

"And that powder keg in Chicago set off a riot that went on for five days," Toby said.

"Yes," Gressley said grimly. "By the time it was over, twenty-three Negroes and fifteen whites had been killed, and nearly three hundred others were injured. It's up to us to make sure something like that doesn't happen here. One thing we can do to help is conduct a thorough investigation so we don't make a false arrest. We also don't want to aggravate anybody unnecessarily."

"Is that why we're not going to interview Leroy at the factory?"

"That's right. We don't want to jeopardize his job or contribute to some wild rumor. I was told that he usually walks down Twenty-fourth Street when he goes home. We'll just wait until he's a couple of blocks away from the factory before we approach him. Also, since you have a uniform on, it might be best if you stay in the car."

Toby nodded toward the factory. "They're coming out now."

Moments later Leroy Beckwith was seen walking down Twenty-fourth Street. As he approached the policemen, Gressley slid out of the car. "Leroy Beckwith?"

Leroy stopped and looked at Gressley cautiously. "Yeah, that's me."

Gressley introduced himself. "I'd like to ask you some questions about Russell Wilcox's murder. We can just keep walking while we talk."

"I wondered how long it would be before you wanted to see me. I didn't do it."

"I was told you held a grudge against Russell."

Leroy grunted. "I was pretty upset when Lillie Mae dumped me, and I probably said some things I shouldn't have. But that's all over now. I got a new girl-friend in Flint."

"What's her name?"

"Nellie Johnson."

"Were you with her Saturday night?"

"Yes."

Gressley said, "I'll need her address and phone number to verify your story. What time did you leave Port Huron?"

Leroy gave Gressley the address and phone number. He said, "I took the six o'clock train Saturday, and didn't come back until Sunday night."

"What did you do in Flint?"

"We went to Rooney's Club and listened to ragtime and jazz. It was mostly songs by Eubie Blake."

"What were some of the songs?"

Leroy thought for a moment. "Let's see … 'Charleston Rag,' 'Baltimore Buzz,' 'Messin' Around,' 'I'm Just Simply Full of Jazz,' 'I'm Just Wild about Harry'—"

Gressley stopped him. "Do you know Rodney Beckwith?"

"Yeah. That's my cousin from Flint. He and his girlfriend were at the club with us Saturday night. Why do you want to know about Rodney?"

"He was arrested by the Port Huron police last summer for stealing a car."

Leroy asked, "What would that have to do with Russell's murder?"

"Are you and Rodney close?"

"I don't know what you're gettin' at, but I didn't help him steal that car, and he wasn't in Port Huron on Saturday."

Gressley stopped walking. "Just one more thing. Would you pick up your feet so I can see the bottoms of your shoes?"

Leroy complied.

After Gressley took a look, he said, "Thanks. That will be all for now."

As Gressley slid into the car, Toby asked, "What did he say?"

"He claims he was in Flint on Saturday night. Let's go to the depot to see if we can confirm that."

"Will do." Toby headed toward the Grand Trunk Railroad Depot.

"You were right about Rodney Beckwith," Gressley said. "They're cousins. Leroy said they were both with their girlfriends at a place called Rooney's Club the night Russell was murdered."

"I've heard about it. Some of the best ragtime and jazz musicians in the country play there."

Toby parked in the depot lot. The pair entered the depot and walked to the ticket window.

Gressley showed his identification to the ticket agent and asked, "Were you working Saturday night?"

"Yes, sir. I worked from four to midnight."

"Do you remember selling a ticket to a young Negro man? He's about five feet ten inches tall, slim, and he has a moustache."

The ticket agent said, "Yep. I sold him a round-trip ticket. I think his name is Leroy. He's been buying tickets to Flint nearly every weekend."

"Did you see him get on the train?"

"No. I was pretty busy; I didn't pay attention to who boarded."

Gressley said, "Thanks."

As they walked to the car, Gressley said, "We know he bought a ticket, but we don't know for sure if he actually got on the train. If he was planning a murder, that might be a good way to have an alibi."

Toby looked at his watch. "Are we going to do anything else today?"

"No. Just drop me off at home. Do you have something planned?"

"I promised to take the family downtown. Amanda has play practice at the Majestic at six o'clock. Are you going to see the play?"

"Yes. Sylvia and I have tickets for Saturday night."

CHAPTER 22

▼

Graham Hastings stood across the street from the Majestic Theater, hidden from view. He had prepared carefully for tonight. If Mary Sharpe's husband stayed for the rehearsal, Graham would use a clever ploy to separate them. From past experience he knew this could be challenging, but he had no doubt in his ability to succeed. Of course, the evening would be easier if Mary's husband did not stay at the theater.

Once he had Mary alone, Graham was confident he could convince her to accompany him to the Harrington Hotel. Until he had called her that afternoon, he had not assumed that would be a problem. He straightened his tie, knowing that it would take all of his finely honed charms to seduce Mary.

Being the consummate planner, Graham had also made preparations to leave town quickly. He enjoyed cuckolding husbands, but he had no interest in fighting them. He had packed his suitcase and checked the train schedule to see what his post-eight o'clock options were. There were only two—a nine o'clock train to Chicago and a ten o'clock train to Detroit. He looked at his watch impatiently. It was nearing six o'clock.

*   *   *   *

Toby parked the family car on Huron Avenue. As his family got out of the car, Amanda asked, "Daddy, are you going to watch the rehearsal?"

Toby held Amanda's hand as they turned to begin walking down Grand River Avenue.

"Chris and I are going to do a few errands first. We should be back for the second hour."

Mary, holding a knitting basket, asked, "What are you going to do?" She thought, *I hope he isn't planning to sit in his car and drink.*

Chris said, "Daddy promised me I could get a new bag of marbles."

Toby nodded his head, "Yep. Somehow Chris lost his favorite shooter. Then I'm going to stop at Springer and Rose to see if the tailor is finished with the new suit I bought. I've been so busy with the murder case; I haven't had a chance to pick it up."

Mary looked at Chris. "Are you going to have time to work on your Underground Railroad report?"

Chris said, "I've got it here in my knapsack. I'll get busy as soon as Dad and I are done."

As the family approached the theater entrance, Amanda let go of her dad's hand. She pointed to a girl waiting at the door. "That's Rosa. She's my friend in the play."

Amanda ran into the theater to catch up with Rosa.

Mary kissed her husband on the cheek and followed her daughter into the theater. She sat in the back and began knitting.

*   *   *   *

Graham watched as Mary and her daughter entered the theater. He then heard Toby Sharpe say to his son, "Let's go to Bingham's Hardware Store first. Then we'll check on my suit." Graham hurried into the theater and looked for Mary. He found her sitting alone.

Graham sat down beside Mary and lightly touched her arm. He smiled. "Evenin', Mary."

Mary jumped. "How did you get in here?"

"Same as you. I wanted to continue the little chat we were having this afternoon."

Graham and Mary momentarily turned their attention to the stage where Clara Sibella stood earnestly talking to her cast. "This is one of our last rehearsals before Friday's opening night performance, so I hope everyone's ready to work hard tonight." She turned to face the visitors. "I want all of you to be as quiet as possible. The actors are not to be distracted."

Graham whispered, "My offer to go to the Harrington still stands."

"I won't go," Mary chided as she glared at Graham. "You'd better leave. My husband and son will be back soon."

Graham ignored her. "I heard them say they had several errands to run. We could leave now. When you return, you can simply say that you had to run an errand of your own." He looked at her knitting basket. "Maybe you had to get more yarn."

Mary's voice rose. "I told you no. Please leave me alone."

Several people in the front of the theater turned to look at them. The director said sternly, "Would visitors please be quiet, or leave."

Graham whispered, "Keep your voice down. You're going to embarrass your daughter. Let's discuss this in the lobby."

Mary sighed. She did not want to continue the conversation, but she was also afraid that if she remained in the theater she would disrupt rehearsal. She set her knitting down and followed Graham to the lobby.

*   *   *   *

Chris put his new bag of marbles in his knapsack as he and his dad entered Springer and Rose. "Thanks again, Dad. These are really nice."

Pete Richmond stopped straitening a stack of shirts and smiled.

Toby said, "Hi, Pete. I'd like to pick up my new suit tonight."

"Let me see if it's ready." Pete disappeared into a back room for a few minutes. When he reappeared, he was frowning. "Jeez, I'm sorry. One of the tailors has been under the weather so they're a little behind. It should be ready by noon tomorrow."

"No problem. I'll pick it up after work."

Toby and Chris left the store and headed for the Majestic Theater.

*   *   *   *

It became increasing clear to Graham that Mary was not going to join him at the Harrington Hotel. Out of desperation he pulled Mary to him and leaned over to kiss her.

Mary, fearful of being seen or heard, struggled to get free.

Graham held her tighter.

Mary whispered, "Let me go."

"I don't want to hurt you. Come to my room."

"No!"

*   *   *   *

Toby and Chris stood outside the theater door. Toby said, "I have a few more things to do. You go on in and finish your homework."

"OK, Dad. See you later." As Chris entered the lobby he saw two figures in the far corner. One was a stranger, but he recognized the other as his mother. Not knowing what to do, he hid behind a column and watched as Mary dug the heel of her shoe into the stranger's foot. When the man released his hold, Mary ran into the theater. The man looked at his shoe, and whined, "Look at that scratch. What did she do that for?"

As the stranger limped out of the lobby, he failed to notice Chris hiding behind the column. Chris opened his knapsack and removed the slingshot and large shooter marble he had just purchased.

Chris snuck out of the theater being careful to remain as quiet as possible. Once outside, he saw the stranger walking toward Huron Avenue. Chris loaded his slingshot, aimed it at the man's back, and ran in his direction. As soon as he'd fired, he turned right and ran down the alley behind the buildings facing Huron Avenue. He grinned when he heard a yell from behind him.

Chris ran into Springer and Rose. He grabbed a pair of pants, waved them at Pete, and yelled, "I want to try these on!" as he ducked into a fitting room. Once inside, he sat on a stool, pulled his knees up to his chin, and closed his eyes. His body shook with fear and excitement.

*   *   *   *

Moments later, Graham Hastings entered the clothing store rubbing his right shoulder.

"Did anyone just run in here?"

Pete set down a pile of shirts, consciously not looking in the direction of the fitting room where Chris was hiding. "Not in the past fifteen minutes."

Graham looked around the store, then turned and stalked out the door.

Pete went to the front door and looked around. Graham Hastings was not in sight. Pete walked over to the fitting room. "He's gone. You can come out now."

Chris looked at his slingshot. He wanted to take it with him, but he remembered his dad talking about the importance of evidence. Chris rubbed the slingshot for good luck before sliding it inside the pants he had taken into the fitting room. He exited the fitting room and laid the pants on a shelf. "Guess I don't want these. They're too big."

Pete asked, "Why did you come into the store? I don't think you wanted to buy any pants."

Chris glanced at the door. Talking quickly, he said, "My sister's practicing her play. I got bored, so I just left the theater for a while."

Peter rubbed his large nose, and looked closely at the obviously frightened boy. "Now tell me the truth, Chris. Did you do something to that man?"

Chris looked down at his hands. "He's a bad man."

"What do you mean?"

Chris pressed his lips together, refusing to say anything else.

Pete signaled his boss. "Do you mind if I leave a few minutes early? I have an errand."

"Go ahead; we don't have any customers right now anyway."

Turning to Chris, Pete said, "I'm going in the direction of the theater. How about we walk together?"

Chris nodded. "OK."

Once outside, they walked in silence for several minutes. Finally, Pete said, "The sky's sure clear tonight. I like to look for constellations on nights like this. Do you know what the Big Dipper looks like?"

Chris opened the door to the theater. "You mean the Drinking Gourd?" He smiled as he made the connection between the Big Dipper and the Negro spiritual that Clayton Boyd had told him about. "So that makes the owners of your store stationmasters. And you're a conductor who saved me from a slave catcher. Thanks for bringing me to freedom!"

Pete watched as Chris ran into the theater. He shook his head and muttered, "What the heck was that all about?"

*   *   *   *

After dropping Chris off at the theater, Toby's initial impulse was to drive to Pine Grove Park and take a few nips from his whiskey flask. But as he waited to cross Huron Avenue, a more compelling thought arose. He walked to his car and was soon headed to the north end of town.

Toby had never visited his daughter's grave by himself. In fact, he had come to resent Mary's insistence that they visit almost daily. But he had been thinking about Natalie ever since his conversation with Chris on Saturday. Now here he was, driving to Lakeside Cemetery.

He turned into the cemetery and parked in front of the memorial for the soldiers who died of the cholera epidemic in 1832. He slid out of the car, walked to Natalie's grave, and knelt in front of her tombstone. Using his fingers, he traced the letters carved in the stone.

Toby recalled how much Natalie liked birds, especially cardinals. Toby smiled, remembering that Natalie had called them car-dals. She had even learned to imitate the cardinals' song. She would wave her arms, and say, "Look, Daddy, I'm a car-dal." Then she would sing, "What-cheer-cheer-cheer."

Toby stood up and wiped the dirt from his pants. He said, "I love you, dear Natalie." He turned and began to walk toward his car when suddenly he heard a familiar sound—"What-cheer-cheer-cheer."

He whirled around to see a bright red cardinal perched on Natalie's tombstone. The bird cocked its head and looked directly at Toby before flying to a nearby bush. Toby stood for a few moments, finally releasing the tears of grief he had contained for so long.

Toby returned to the Majestic Theater and sat with his family for the remainder of the rehearsal. When it was over, they crawled into the car for the drive home. Amanda chattered unceasingly about the play, the director, and her new friend, Rosa. Toby, Mary, and Chris sat quietly.

CHAPTER 23

▼

It was early Wednesday morning, and Gressley was already finishing his second cigarette of the day. He was ruminating on the difficulty he was having trying to stop smoking when Toby entered his office. Toby sat down and asked, "Where do we start today?"

"Let's reconsider our suspects."

"Well," said Toby, "we got the four guys at the lumberyard who didn't like Russell. They all claim they were playing poker together Saturday night, but no one outside of their group can either support or deny their story. So they have a motive, and they might have had opportunity."

"Who do you think was the weakest member of that group?"

Toby thought for a moment. "I would say Hank Peters. You said he seemed pretty nervous when you talked to him Monday."

"I agree. We should go back and talk to him again."

"What do you think about Leroy Beckwith's story? It seems like he has two possible motives for killing Russell—his jealousy over losing Lillie Mae and the stolen car incident."

Gressley said, "He needs to stay on our list of suspects, but I don't see why he would get people from Flint to come to Port Huron just because Russell didn't get punished for stealing the car last summer. And if it's true that Leroy's got a girlfriend in Flint, the jealousy issue doesn't make much sense either."

"What about the four men Oscar Danbridge saw Friday night? It's interesting that Luke Laboy only told us where he and his brother were Saturday night. He didn't give an alibi for Mike Sweeney or the other man in the car. Maybe we ought to find them."

Gressley opened the Port Huron City Directory that was lying on his desk. "That's where we're going to start today. I found five Sweeneys listed. I want you to visit each family and find out if there's a Mike Sweeney in his mid-twenties in any of the households." He shoved the directory across the desk to Toby. "While you're doing that, I'm going to Farmer and Conselyea's shoe store to talk to Dave Hanton about shoes."

"You think they might be able to identify the odd heel mark?"

"If it's unique enough, he might recognize it. He might even know the names of people who would buy such a heel."

Toby stood up. "Where should I meet you when I'm done visiting the Sweeneys?"

"Come back here when you're done. Then we're going to the Harrington Hotel for lunch."

"The Harrington Hotel? Isn't that a pretty expensive place to have lunch?"

Gressley laughed softly. "I talked to Bill Boyd this morning. He wants to meet us for lunch. He suggested the Harrington because he had some business to do in that part of town."

"Are you going to tell him anything about the murder? You know he's going to ask."

Gressley smiled. "We'll see. Maybe he'll be able to help us in some way."

Toby and Gressley exited the building together. Gressley watched as Toby got in the Model T and drove off. Gressley then buttoned his overcoat as protection from the blustery fall wind and set off on foot toward Water Street.

Minutes later, Gressley entered the shoe store and was struck with the pungent smells of leather, glue, and cigar smoke. He saw a short man in his early thirties at a workbench, a cigar in his mouth. The man spoke in a thick Scottish brogue. "Detective Gressley. Your shoes in need of repair so soon?"

"No. But I'd like to ask you some questions about shoes."

Dave Hanton laughed. "I hope you're not plannin' to make a career change. If so, I'll tell you to get out right now. I have too much competition already."

Gressley removed a photograph from his suit pocket. "I'll leave shoe repairs to the experts." He handed the photo to Hanton. "Do you recognize the marking on the heel of this shoe?"

"Aye. It's for people who wear down the side of their heels, but don't want to wear a metal plate on their shoe. I have to special order them."

"How often do you do that?"

Hanton thought for a moment. "Oh, I'd say about once a month."

"Could you tell me the names of anyone who's ordered them?"

Hanton pointed to a cabinet along the back wall. "We have records for the past six months in there. But all the orders are mixed together. It would take a while to find the ones you want."

"How long?"

"I could have my kids help me when they get in the house after school today."

"Could I pick the list up first thing tomorrow morning?"

Hanton nodded. "I'll have it ready for you."

*   *   *   *

When Toby returned to the police station, he found Gressley in his office studying the rope used to hang Russell Wilcox. Toby could not recall ever seeing a rope quite like the one on Gressley's desk. It was white with small, but extremely strong, fibers. Gressley looked up when he sensed Toby standing at the door. He put the rope in a desk drawer and waved Toby into the office.

Gressley asked, "Were you able to talk to all the Sweeney families?"

Toby sat down. "Yep. And I found two Mikes. One is only nine years old, so I doubt if he's our 'man.'"

"I think you're probably right. What about the other one?"

"I talked to his mother. She didn't want to say a whole lot. It seems that Mike and his dad had a terrible argument about two years ago. Mike was kicked out of the house, and he left Port Huron. His mother's heard rumors that he's back in town, but she swears she hasn't seen him."

"What did he and his dad argue about?"

"Mrs. Sweeney wouldn't say."

"How old is he?"

"Twenty-four," Toby replied.

"Has he ever been arrested?"

"I looked him up in the files, but couldn't find anything about him."

"Sounds like we need to check out the hotels and boardinghouses to see if he's in town."

"What did you find out at the shoe store?" Toby asked.

"Mr. Hanton says the marking signifies a special heel used by people who wear out the side of their regular heel. He has to special order them. He's going to give us a list of names of people who have ordered them during the past six months." Gressley stood up and put on his overcoat. "It's time for lunch."

*   *   *   *

Bill Boyd was waiting in the lobby of the Harrington Hotel when the two policemen arrived. He shook Gressley's hand. "Nice to see you again, detective." Leading the way, Bill said, "I reserved a nice quiet table in the corner."

Once they were seated, Bill continued, "I was disappointed when I called the police station and didn't hear the familiar voice of Sylvia Pointe."

"She joined the Red Cross Motor Corps during the war. When she came back, she got a job at the Woman's Benefit Association," Gressley said.

"What's she doing there?"

Gressley said, "She's visiting several cities this week, talking to women about registering to vote."

Bill asked, "What cities is she visiting?"

"Lapeer, Flint, Rochester, and Oaks Corner. She'll be back in Port Huron on Saturday."

Toby said, "Maybe Sylvia's dream of becoming a policewoman won't happen, but at least she's happy about women getting the right to vote."

Bill turned to Gressley. "Now that she's no longer working for the police department, is there a wedding in the future?"

Gressley studied his menu for a moment, then he looked at Bill. "Yes. Sylvia and I plan to get married sometime, but we haven't set a date yet. How's your uncle doing?"

Before Bill could answer, a waiter appeared to take their orders. After the waiter left, Bill said, "He gets tired easily. But in some ways he looks better than he did the last time I saw him. He's on a diet and he's started exercising. He has a housekeeper who comes to the house every day. She helps him a lot."

Toby said, "I hope my son wasn't a nuisance Monday."

"Good Lord, no. Uncle Clayton had a great time. You know how he likes to use his files."

Gressley arched his eyebrows. "What files?"

Toby laughed. "Clayton has file cabinets filled with all kinds of information in his study."

Bill said, "He used to bore us to death when we were young. He'd corner us in his study and ask, 'Who would like to hear about the great children's blizzard of 1888?'"

"But a lot of the things he talked about were interesting." Toby said. "I know Chris really got caught up in listening about the Underground Railroad."

The waiter returned with their meals and asked, "Is there anything else you would like?"

Gressley shook his head, "This is fine."

Toby chewed on his roast beef sandwich for a few moments. Then he asked, "Are you planning to stay in Port Huron permanently to run the paper?"

"I'm not sure," Bill said. "It depends largely on how well my uncle recovers."

Toby asked, "Have you found anyone to date since you've been back? I doubt if you have as many choices as you did in Philadelphia."

Bill said. "As a matter of fact, I have a date tonight with Edna Bryant. She helps her aunt take care of my uncle. We're going to see that Colleen Moore movie showing at the Maxine."

Toby laughed. "You're taking a girl to see a baseball movie?"

"That shows how much you know. It turns out she is a Chicago White Sox fan, so I sure we'll have a lot of fun." Bill reached into his inside suit pocket, took out a sheet of paper, and laid it on the table. "Here's something I want to ask you about. I found this in my uncle's office. He had wadded it up and thrown it away. Apparently he missed the wastebasket and it wasn't picked up with the trash."

Gressley looked at the paper. "Oh, that's an announcement for Friday night's meeting of the Whitecaps of America. Someone posted one of these at the police station, but Chief Chambers tore it down."

"I've never heard of the Whitecaps. Are they something like the Ku Klux Klan?"

"Sounds pretty similar to me," Toby said. He pointed at the bottom of the paper. "Look at this. For ten dollars, you get a year's membership and a uniform. It looks like their meeting is near Oaks Corner."

Gressley grabbed the paper. "Did you say Oaks Corner? I didn't pay much attention to it when it was on the bulletin board. Sylvia's going to be there Friday night."

Bill sighed, "Oh, boy. That's going to be interesting. Putting her near a racist rally would be like throwing a match into a gasoline tank."

Toby said, "I'm sure she'll be careful." The three men looked at each other knowing that being careful was not a trait Sylvia Pointe possessed.

The waiter returned to clear their dishes. He asked, "Would any of you like dessert?"

Gressley said, "Just some more coffee for me." The other two nodded in agreement.

Bill said, "Before you two leave, you know I have to ask you about the murder investigation. How are things going?"

Gressley said, "We're still tracking down suspects."

"Do you have any leads that haven't been in the paper?"

"We have a few, but we don't want them published," Gressley said. "But I do have a question about your uncle's files."

"What about them?"

"Can I tell you something about the murder that you promise will remain off the record?"

Bill said, "Sure. But what does it have to do with my uncle's files?"

"The rope used to hang Russell Wilcox is different than any we have ever seen. The owner of the lumberyard said it might be something used in a Wild West show or a circus."

Bill slapped his knee. "By George! The circus is one of my uncle's favorite topics. He's got all kinds of articles about Barnum & Bailey and other circuses. He'd be happy to share them."

Gressley turned to Toby. "I'm going to Russell's funeral this afternoon. I want you to see if Clayton has any information that might help us."

Bill asked, "Any instructions for me?"

"Perhaps you could write an article requesting anyone who has any information to contact the police."

The three men stood up. Bill offered a military salute. "Yes, sir. Consider it done."

CHAPTER 24

▼

Toby knocked on Clayton Boyd's front door. A middle-aged woman with a sweet smile answered. "Good afternoon, officer. How can I help you?"

Toby introduced himself. "I'm a good friend of Bill Boyd's. I was wondering if I could talk to his uncle for a few minutes."

Matilda Bryant moved to the side to allow Toby to enter the house. "He's in his study. He just finished eating his lunch. I'm sure he would like some company."

Toby heard Clayton's voice. "Who's out there?"

"Patrolman Toby Sharpe. He would like to talk to you," Matilda said.

Clayton greeted Toby at the door to his study. "Nice to have you drop by. I had the most interesting conversation with your son a couple days ago. Come on in and sit down. Would you like some tea?"

"That sure sounds good on a chilly day like today. It feels like we're going to have an early winter."

Clayton turned to Matilda. "Please fix this young man a pot of steaming hot tea."

Matilda nodded and headed for the kitchen.

Toby looked at Clayton closely. He agreed with Bill's assessment about his uncle. Clayton appeared smaller, but in some ways he looked healthier than he did before his heart attack.

Clayton asked, "What brings you here in the middle of a workday?"

Toby showed Clayton a photograph of the rope that was used to hang Russell Wilcox. "This is the rope that was used to hang Russell Wilcox. We were told it might be the type that would have been used in a Wild West show or a circus. I was wondering if you could help us identify it."

Clayton pointed to the third filing cabinet from the corner. "If you open the second drawer in that cabinet, you'll see a bunch of folders about circuses. Bring them over here to the coffee table and we'll see what we've got. Oh, and bring that magnifying glass from the desk."

As Toby put the folders on the coffee table, Clayton took a closer look at the photograph.

Clayton said, "You know what? I don't think this will be too difficult."

Clayton noticed Matilda approaching the door. "Ah, just bring that right in."

Matilda set a tray holding a teapot, cups, milk, and sugar on the coffee table beside the folders. She said, "I'll be leaving now. I've fixed your supper, and put it in the ice box. Remember, Edna won't be coming over tonight."

Clayton smiled. "That's right. Bill is going to take her to the movies. I'll see you tomorrow morning."

Toby poured his tea and added some milk. "I heard about Bill's date. What's Edna like?"

"She's tall and slender, blue eyes … and she has a great personality."

Toby thought, *I wonder whose idea it was to date Edna—Bill's or his uncle's. Bill doesn't look for girls with great personalities.*

Toby picked up one of the folders. "Are these arranged chronologically?"

"For the most part. There's a special section on P. T. Barnum that has more than just circus material. Here's a poster about Jenny Lind, the Swedish Nightingale, when she toured the United States under Barnum's management in 1850. Here's a photograph of The Barnum Museum when the confederates tried to burn it down in 1864."

Toby sipped his tea hoping that Clayton would finally get around to talking about circus ropes.

Clayton, unaware of Toby's impatience, continued. "Here's a Barnum's program from 1871, the year Barnum opened what he dubbed 'The Greatest Show on Earth.' Do you know it's a myth that he said 'there's a sucker born every minute?'" Clayton paused and looked at Toby's blank expression. "But I don't suppose you want to know about P. T. Barnum, do you?"

"Maybe some other time. I'm really interested in what you know about ropes."

Clayton picked up one of the folders. "This has the most recent information." He removed six circus posters and laid them on the table next to the photograph

Toby had handed him. Clayton asked, "Do you see any similarities between the rope in the photo and the ropes in the circus posters?"

Toby looked carefully. He shook his head. "No."

Clayton removed three of the posters. "What do these three have that the others don't?"

Toby clapped his hands. "The ropes on the trapeze swings!" He took the magnifying glass from Clayton and looked at the posters more carefully. "They look like the rope in the photo."

Clayton leaned back placing the tips of his fingers together. Assuming an English accent, he said, "Elementary, my dear Toby. Perhaps you are looking for someone who worked for a circus."

Toby laughed. "Thanks, Sherlock."

CHAPTER 25

▼

Gressley stubbed out a cigarette before entering the Mount Olive Baptist Church. Inside the church, he stood for a moment looking at the people who had assembled. He saw a few white faces, including Mr. and Mrs. Stockwell.

Gressley was trying to decide where to sit when he heard a familiar voice behind him. He turned to see Oscar Danbridge. Oscar extended his hand. "Detective Gressley, glad to see you could make it. This is my wife, Rachel."

Gressley smiled at Rachel. "Pleased to meet you." Facing Oscar he said, "It's the least I could do. Looks like a large turnout."

"Russell was a popular young man. He made friends with almost everyone. Are you with anyone?"

"No."

Oscar pointed at an empty pew. "You can sit with me if you'd like. Rachel is part of the program."

"That would be great."

A few minutes after they were seated, Russell Wilcox's family entered the church and sat in the front pews. The congregation rose and sang "Steal Away to Jesus." Gressley sensed an emotional rhythm that did not occur in his church.

The Reverend James Mayes walked to the pulpit. In a sonorous voice he said, "Please remain standing while we pray." He raised his hands above his head. Most of the parishioners did the same as they swayed back and forth.

"Blessed Lord, have mercy on our souls."

"Mercy!"

"And please, if it be Your will …"

"Your will!"

"provide a place in heaven ..."

"Please, Lord!"

"for a beloved member of out community, Russell Wilcox. Amen."

"Amen!"

As the congregation sat down, Freeda Wilcox exploded in grief, collapsing into her daughters' loving arms.

Gressley felt saddened as he looked at the anguished expressions on the faces of Russell's family and friends. His attention returned to the pulpit when he heard Reverend Mayes say, "Please listen to the beautiful voice of Rachel Danbridge as she sings 'Precious Lord.'"

Many continued to cry as Rachel's rich soprano voice filled the room.

When she finished, Reverend Mayes said, "Praise the Lord. Thank you, sister Rachel. And Russell thanks you too. We know he's smiling down at us from heaven above."

"Amen!"

"We know that the Lord has taken Russell's hand and welcomed him into Glory land."

"Glory land!"

Reverend Mayes delivered a stirring eulogy, complimenting Russell Wilcox for being a loving son and a credit to his community. The service concluded with the congregation singing "Swing Low, Sweet Chariot." Gressley continued to be impressed with the spirited service.

He walked beside Oscar Danbridge as the congregation filed out. Gressley said, "Your wife has an outstanding voice."

"Thanks. She considered becoming a professional singer, but marriage and children kind of got in the way."

"I was wondering if we could talk a little when we get outside."

"Is this about the murder?"

"Yes. Maybe we could walk down to the corner to get away from the crowd."

Once they reached the corner, Gressley said, "I have a couple of questions about Leroy Beckwith. What can you tell me about his private life?"

"I know he was really upset when he and Lillie Mae broke up. But his mother told me that he had a new girlfriend. It's my understanding that he's planning to marry her and move to Flint."

Gressley asked, "Do you know anything about his girlfriend, Nellie Johnson?"

"I've never met her."

"Would you happen to know what kind of music he likes?"

Oscar said, "He's always talking about ragtime and jazz when he comes into the store. He really likes Eubie Blake. And anyway, I heard that he left town Saturday night for Flint."

"Is there anyone who might confirm that?"

Oscar pointed to a man emerging from the church. "That's Sylvester Jackson. He works in the dining room on the train between here and Chicago. He might have seen Leroy."

They stood quietly for a moment, then Oscar said, "I want to thank you for coming today. Black people are on edge about what's happening, and it was good to see the police showing some interest in what goes on in our community."

Gressley said, "Thanks. I know things have been pretty bad this year with all of the lynching and riots around the country."

"It seems like things are getting worse instead of better. Most Negroes voted for Woodrow Wilson in 1912. Then he turns around and segregates federal employees and cuts back the number of Negroes in civil service."

"I know. It seems like the federal government has turned its back on what little progress had been made."

Oscar said bitterly, "One of the worst things President Wilson did was make those stupid comments about that rotten movie, *The Birth of a Nation.* I couldn't believe he said that the movie was 'like writing history with lightening,' and that his only regret was 'that it is all terribly true.' I can tell you, he didn't get my vote in the 1916 election."

Gressley nodded. "Let's hope that someday things will change." Gressley excused himself as he watched Sylvester Jackson begin to walk away from the church. "I want to talk to that man before he leaves."

Gressley approached Sylvester quickly and introduced himself. "Were you working the Port Huron-to-Chicago route Saturday night?"

"Yes, sir."

"Do you remember seeing Leroy Beckwith on that train?"

Sylvester nodded.

"Are you sure it was last Saturday?"

"Yes, because we talked about the Michigan vs. Ohio State football game that was played that afternoon."

CHAPTER 26

▼

Toby entered the police station and was headed toward Gressley's office when Mabel, the new secretary, beckoned him to her desk. She said, "Detective Gressley left you this note, and your wife would like you to call her when you have a minute."

Toby looked at the note. It read, "I called the Harrington Hotel, the Hotel Marion, the Prince Albert Hotel, and the Gratiot Inn to see if any of them had registered a Mike Sweeney. None had. Would you continue to call hotels and boardinghouses when you get back? Use the city directory and phone in my office. And please pick me up at my apartment tomorrow at seven thirty."

Toby sat at Gressley's desk and called home.

"Hello."

"Hi, Mary. You wanted me to call?"

Mary paused for a moment. "Are you alone?"

"Yes. I'm in Gressley's office."

"I ... I just need to tell you what happened last night in the theater while you were gone. I felt so ashamed when we got home last night; I couldn't talk about it. Maybe we could talk when you get home tonight."

Toby frowned as he thought about his visit to the cemetery. Finally he said, "Sure, we can talk tonight. I have something to share too. I should be home by five o'clock. Maybe we can talk after supper."

"Fine. Toby, I love you very much."

Toby smiled. "I love you too." As he thought about Mary's call, he remembered that his son had been unusually quiet on the ride home from the theater. At the time, he assumed Chris was probably going through a stage. But now, he wondered if it might have been something else. *Whatever is going on, it will have to wait until I get home.* Reaching for the city directory, he began the monotonous process of phoning hotels and boardinghouses.

An hour later, Toby hung up the receiver and rubbed his ear. He had called ten more places since talking with Gressley with no luck. Closing the directory, he thought, *I've done enough of this for the day.*

Toby said good-bye to Mabel and walked to Springer and Rose. Pete Richmond looked up as Toby entered the store. Pete said, "Your suit's ready." He hurried to the back room, and reemerged with Toby's suit. "Use the dressing room on the right."

Toby put the suit on and looked in the mirror. Everything fit well. He took the suit off and handed it back to Pete. He said, "It fits great."

Pete slipped a bag over the suit and took Toby's money. Then he placed a slingshot on the counter.

Toby looked at the slingshot. "What's this for?"

Pete coughed. "It belongs to your son. I found it in a pair of pants last night."

"Why would he put it there?"

"Remember when the two of you were in the store about six o'clock?"

Toby nodded.

"Well, about twenty minutes later he came running into the store and hid in one of the dressing rooms. Then a man charged in looking for someone. He was rubbing his shoulder like he had been hit with something."

"You think Chris hit him with the slingshot?"

Pete said, "I think so. Chris came out of the dressing room after the man left. He said the man was bad, but he wouldn't explain what he meant. I could tell he was really scared. So I walked him to the Majestic. When we got to the theater, he started babbling about drinking gourds and conductors. I didn't know what he was talking about."

"I'll find out. Thanks for telling me." Toby grabbed his suit and the slingshot and headed back to the police station to get his car.

*   *   *   *

As soon as Toby arrived home, he stormed into the kitchen and asked, "Where's Chris?"

She nodded toward the stairway. "He went to his room as soon as he got home from school. He acted like he was upset. I thought something was bothering him last night, and now I'm sure of it. I tried to talk to him today, but he wouldn't say anything. I should have talked to him before he went to bed last night, but I was too preoccupied."

"Preoccupied about what?"

"We'll talk later. Maybe you should talk to Chris first."

Toby bound up the stairs and entered Chris's room. The boy was lying on his bed. Toby showed him the slingshot. "Do you mind telling me how this got in a pair of pants at Springer and Rose?"

Chris's eyes widened. "How did you get that?"

"Pete Richmond gave it to me when I picked up my suit. Now answer my question."

"I hit a man with it."

Toby voice rose. "What? Why in the devil did you do that?"

Chris sniffed. "Because he's bad."

Toby sat down on Chris's bed. He spoke sternly. "That's what Pete said you told him. Would you please tell me what happened?"

Chris nervously rubbed his hands on the bedspread, then spoke hesitantly. "When you dropped me off at the theater, I saw a man hurting Mom."

"Hurting her?"

"Yeah. He was holding her and she was trying to get free."

"Good God. What did your mother do?"

Chris relaxed slightly. In a stronger voice, he said, "Mom was great. You should have seen her. She stomped on his foot. After that, Mom went back to sit down and the man left the theater."

"And you followed him?"

"Yeah. I used the run, shoot, and run maneuver with the slingshot. You know, the way I showed you Saturday."

Toby held Chris's hand. "But you know you shouldn't have done that, don't you? You could have gotten into serious trouble."

Chris nodded. "I know. And I was really scared afterward. But he was hurting Mom. I didn't say anything last night because I thought you and Mom would be angry."

Toby clasped Chris's shoulders. "You did a brave thing. I might have done the same thing in that situation. What did this man look like?"

"He was tall, parted his hair in the middle, and had a small moustache. He kinda looked like Douglas Fairbanks."

"The movie actor?"

"Yeah."

Toby stood up. "One other thing, Pete said you talked about drinking gourds and conductors. What do they have to do with what happened?"

Chris laughed. "Those were words used by slaves when they took the Underground Railroad. I learned them from Mr. Boyd."

Chris wanted to continue to talk about the Underground Railroad, but Toby interrupted him. "Some other time. Right now I need to talk to your mother."

Toby returned to the kitchen. Mary was sitting at the table, pealing potatoes. He said, "I just had an interesting conversation with our son."

Mary looked up. "Did you find out what was bothering him?"

Toby sat down at the table. "I sure did. He said he saw someone hurting you last night."

Mary put the paring knife down and rubbed her throat. "Good heavens. He saw that?"

"When were you going to tell me about it?"

"Tonight. That's why I called you today at work. I wanted to tell you last night, but I was too embarrassed."

Toby asked, "Who was he? Do I know him?"

"His name is Milton Burks. He was trying to get me to go to the Harrington Hotel with him. When I refused, he became frustrated. He pulled me into his arms and kissed me."

"Right at the theater?"

Mary looked at Toby, tears brimmed her eyes. "Yes. I was so afraid someone would see us. It would give people something terrible to gossip about. I wouldn't be able to face your mother if that happened."

"Did you know that man before last night?"

Mary wiped her eyes. "I met him at the Blue Bird Club in Detroit last Saturday. He seemed nice, so when he asked me to dance I said yes. But that's all we did."

Toby asked, "How did he know you were from Port Huron?"

"It just came up in the conversation. And I told him about Amanda being in the play. He said he was a traveling salesman and if he ever had any business in Port Huron, he might see me again. But I didn't take him seriously. Then, out of the blue, he called here about two o'clock yesterday and said he wanted to meet me. I said 'no' and hung up on him. I was hoping that was the last I would ever hear from him."

"What does he sell?"

"Uniforms. When I told him you were a policeman, he said many policemen buy his uniforms."

Toby stood up and banged the table with his fist. "I'll show him a uniform! Did you say he was at the Harrington?"

"Yes." As Toby turned to leave, Mary grasped his arm tightly. She pleaded with him, "Please be careful."

*　　　*　　　*　　　*

Toby drove quickly to the Harrington. In less than five minutes, he'd screeched to a stop in front of the hotel. Running up the steps, he gripped the handle of his nightstick. He had never used excessive force, but he thought, *there's a first time for everything. If I could, I would kick him all the way to Detroit.* He grinned as he fantasized Milton Burks's body being catapulted through the air, his arms and legs flailing. Somehow, this absurd image relaxed Toby. By the time he approached the hotel desk, he had released his grip on the nightstick and was able to talk in a relatively normal voice.

The clerk, a young man in his early thirties, asked, "How can I help you, officer?"

"I'm looking for Milton Burks. He checked into your hotel recently."

The clerk looked at the register. "Sorry, we haven't had anyone registered by that name."

Toby could feel his anger returning. "He must be here. He was tall, good-looking. He looked like that actor Douglas Fairbanks."

"Oh, you mean Benjamin Potts. He checked in Monday afternoon and pranced around the place like he owned it. He thought he was the cat's meow."

"Anything else?"

"I remember a phone call he made yesterday at about two o'clock. I couldn't hear the conversation, but he slammed the phone down hard when he was done."

Toby asked, "When did he check out?"

The clerk looked at the guest register. "Seven o'clock last night. He was really in a hurry."

"Where did he say he was going?"

"He said he had to catch a train. I told him the next one didn't leave until nine o'clock, but he said he had some other business to do first."

"Has his room been cleaned?"

The clerk shook his head. "Ordinarily it would be, but the colored woman who cleans that floor requested the afternoon off to attend Russell Wilcox's funeral. I said it was OK if she came back after supper to finish her work."

"Good. Can I have the key? I want to look at that room."
The clerk handed Toby a key. "It's room 209."

CHAPTER 27

▼

Bill Boyd stood in the middle of his bedroom in his underwear and socks. His underwear consisted of a one-piece lightweight union suit made up of a vest-like top and shorts that came nearly to his knees. He finished fastening the last of the six buttons that ran down the front of the union suit. His black socks were firmly secured with garters.

Bill looked at his pale, slim reflection in his dressing mirror, thinking that it might be a good idea if he spent some time next summer outside doing some physical labor. He quickly discounted the idea.

He slipped into his shirt, trousers, and shoes before walking to his closet where he picked out a red bow tie before returning to the dressing mirror. After the third try, his bow tie looked reasonably straight. He picked up his Norfolk jacket with a set-in belt and slung it over his shoulder. Bill thought the informal look of a Norfolk jacket would be appropriate for his movie date with Edna.

He walked downstairs to find his uncle sitting in the living room reading a popular novel about the Great War titled *The Pawns Count,* by E. Phillips Oppenheim. This best-selling book was one of the first twentieth-century novels about international intrigue and espionage. Clayton looked up from his book. "Your tie's crooked."

Bill put on his jacket. "Jeez, I can never get these things to look straight."

Clayton put his book down, stood up, and rubbed his shoulder.

Bill asked, "What's wrong?"

"I'm just a little creaky in the joints." He walked over to Bill and straightened his tie. "There, that looks better."

"Thanks." Bill walked to the coatrack to retrieve his topcoat. "I think I'll need this tonight. It's getting pretty cold."

"You're going to see *The Busher* at the Maxine Theater?"

"That's right. The movie starts at seven. I'll probably be back by eleven."

Clayton said, "Mind your p's and q's with Edna. She's a sweet young girl, and I don't want you making her unhappy."

Bill laughed. "You've got some brass! You practically threw her into my arms Monday night." He put on his expensive wool topcoat with a oxford cut. "Besides, I get the feeling she can take care of herself."

Clayton said, "Just behave yourself."

Bill drove south on Huron Avenue, crossed the Military Street drawbridge, and turned west on Lapeer Avenue. As he drove, he reflected on Port Huron's recent surge in population. The city had increased by nearly ten thousand people in the past five years, with the current population nearing thirty thousand. There had been over five hundred new homes built in the past year alone. The average three bedroom house now sold for one thousand, five hundred dollars.

Bill parked his car in front of the address he was given. Edna's aunt and uncle lived in one of the town's new houses, within walking distance to Mueller's Metals Company where Edna's uncle was employed. Bill slid out of his car, walked to the house, and rang the doorbell.

Matilda Bryant answered. "Good evening, Bill. Edna will be down in a few minutes."

"Hi, Matilda. I want to thank you for taking such good care of my uncle."

Matilda smiled. "He's a pleasure to work for." She looked up the stairs. "Here comes Edna now."

Edna was dressed in a plain black skirt and a white blouse. She carried an inexpensive overcoat. Bill considered Edna's ordinary clothing and felt overdressed. He realized his own clothing was much more expensive than hers.

Bill said, "You look pretty."

Edna smiled as she slipped into her coat. "You look nice, too."

Matilda stood at the door and watched as Bill and Edna walked to the car. She called out, "Have fun," before shutting the door.

Bill and Edna waved, got into the car, and headed for the theater.

CHAPTER 28

▼

The members of the Sharpe family ate their evening meal in silence. Even the normally loquacious Amanda sat quietly eating her food. Each family member stole furtive glances at the others, but no one spoke. When the meal was finished, Mary told the children, "Your father and I need to take a walk. You are to do the dishes."

Eager to break the oppressive silence, Amanda jumped from her chair. "I'll wash. Chris has to dry."

Chris grinned. "That sounds fine to me."

As Amanda and Chris cleared the table, Mary and Toby put on their jackets. Toby held the door for Mary. He asked, "Which way do you want to go?"

"Let's walk toward the water."

After they walked for a few minutes, Mary asked, "What happened at the Harrington Hotel?"

"Milton Burks wasn't there. The clerk said he checked out about seven o'clock last night."

"In some ways, I'm glad you didn't find him. I've never seen you that angry."

"I settled down a little by the time I got to the hotel. Do you know he wasn't even registered as Milton Burks? He was using the name Benjamin Potts," Toby said.

"Are you sure it was the same person?"

"I think so. The clerk agreed that he resembled Douglas Fairbanks. If he used an alias at the hotel, who knows how many more he might have. And that means he might be doing something illegal. So, I took photographs of what seemed to be the most recent fingerprints in his room."

Mary asked, "What can you do with those?"

"There's a group of fingerprint experts in California who are compiling a fingerprint file on criminals. They now have hundreds of thousands of prints. If he's doing something illegal, they might have his prints. I'd like to see if they would check their files."

"Will the department let you do that?"

"I don't know. I'll ask Gressley in the morning."

They stood at the edge of the St. Clair River looking at the rapidly flowing water. Mary pulled her jacket's collar tight around her neck. She glanced down at the sidewalk before looking into Toby's eyes. "I want to tell you everything that happened Saturday night."

Toby turned to watch a freighter heading north. He said cautiously, "OK."

"Rebecca and Frank took me to the Blue Bird Club for dinner. After we were done eating, the two of them decided to dance. I was at the table by myself when Milton Burks introduced himself. We had a pleasant conversation."

Toby picked up a pebble and threw it in the water. "And you danced with him."

"Yes. And I have to admit I was attracted to him. He was handsome and very gentle. I think he was able to affect me in a way I haven't felt for some time."

"So you flirted with him?"

Mary nodded. She whispered, "I guess I did. Then he showed up at the train station Sunday morning."

"He came to Port Huron on Sunday?"

"No. He got off at Oaks Corner. He said he was delivering some uniforms. That's when Bill Boyd saw me. That's also when I decided that I couldn't see Milton Burks again. When he showed up at the theater, I was concerned that someone would see us together."

Toby asked, "What made you concerned? Was it just because you would be embarrassed if someone saw you with him?"

Mary held Toby's hand. "No. I realized how important our relationship is to me. I couldn't risk losing you."

Toby spoke softly. "I don't want to lose you either." After pausing for a moment, he asked, "Do you think he would have hurt you?"

"I don't think so. When I was struggling to get out of his arms he had a mystified look on his face. It was like he couldn't understand why I was rejecting him. But I wasn't afraid he would hurt me."

"I've been thinking about this ever since we talked earlier today. I also remembered what Chris said last Saturday."

Mary looked puzzled. "Chris?"

"He told me you were feeling better, and he was surprised I hadn't noticed. So maybe you were looking for someone who would."

Mary squeezed Toby's hand a little tighter.

As they started walking back to their house, Toby said, "I have a couple of things to share with you."

"What?"

"I visited Natalie's grave by myself last night during Amanda's play practice."

"I wondered where you went."

"You mean because I didn't have alcohol on my breath when I got back?" Toby asked.

Mary nodded.

"Well, that's the other thing I wanted to tell you. I'm going to quit drinking. After all, it's against Michigan law to drink, and it will be a federal crime in a few months."

Mary smiled. "Have you ever gone to Natalie's grave by yourself before?"

Toby shook his head. "While I was there a cardinal sat on her tombstone. I felt like it was singing just to me."

Mary squeezed Toby's hand again. "That's beautiful."

"Then I cried."

"Oh, Toby!"

As they approached their home, Mary said, "Let's sit on the porch swing before we go in the house."

*   *   *   *

Chris and Amanda finished the dishes, and turned to go into the living room when they saw their parents sitting on the porch swing. They watched as Toby put his arm around Mary and she snuggled close to him.

Chris said, "Look at them. They haven't done that in a long time."

"If they kiss, they're going to tell us something important."

"What do you mean?"

Amanda said, "When I was four years old, they did that before they told us there was going to be a baby. And they did the same thing two years ago when they told us they were going to buy a car."

"How do you remember all of that?"

"Because I'm a girl, silly."

Chris groaned. The children became silent, as they watched their parents kiss, first gently, then passionately.

CHAPTER 29

▼

Bill held the door open for Edna as they left the Maxine Theater. "By George, that was a delightful movie," he said.

"You're right. Colleen Moore did a great job. She looks really young. How old is she?"

"She's only nineteen. She was seventeen when she made her first movie."

"And Charles Ray made a convincing carouser," Edna said.

"Have you ever wondered what an actor's voice sounds like?" Speaking falsetto, Bill asked, "What if Charles Ray sounded like this?"

Edna laughed. Using a baritone voice, she said, "I hope that the charming Colleen Moore doesn't talk this low."

They continued to engage in playful banter as they walked toward Bill's car. They were not paying attention to the two men approaching them. Suddenly, one of the men swerved in front of Bill and bumped into him. Bill lost his balance and slipped off the curb. Edna grabbed his coattails to keep him from falling down.

Wilbur Greene smirked. "Good evening, *Mister* Boyd. Having a hard time standing?"

Bill breathed deeply several times before he spoke. "*Patrolman* Greene. At least I assume the police department has been wise enough not to promote you."

Wilbur glared. "Keep your mouth shut, you bag of wind, or I might have to hit you again."

Bill grinned. "Mum's the word."

Wilbur looked at Edna, noticing the inexpensive coat she was wearing. "Who's this, Boyd? Are you slumming?"

Bill's grin disappeared. "You leave her out of this."

Wilbur looked at Edna's long neck. He asked, "Why are you dating *her*? Are you getting desperate?"

As Wilbur spoke, Edna walked slowly toward him, her arms folded across her chest. In her high heels, she was four inches taller than Wilbur. But as she approached him, she seemed to be even taller.

When she was inches away from Wilbur's face, he turned away and muttered, "It's like looking at a damn giraffe."

Bill moved toward Wilbur. "I said to leave her alone."

Wilbur sneered, "What are you going to do, call the cops?"

"I'm sure I could find one that would dignify their position, not abuse it."

As Wilbur drew back his arm to hit Bill, the man with him grabbed it. "Let's go. I want to get some popcorn before the next movie starts."

Wilbur nodded. "OK, Clyde. We can find better company at the theater than we can here on the streets."

Bill and Edna watched the two men walk away. Edna turned to Bill. "Are you OK?"

"He just knocked the wind out of me. I'm sorry he said those things about you."

"I had three brothers that teased me a lot when I was young, so I can handle it. I'll just consider the source. Is that man actually a police officer?"

Bill opened the passenger door of his car. "Unfortunately. But most of the policemen in Port Huron are pleasant enough. If you don't mind me asking, how did you seem so tall when you were standing in front of Wilbur?"

"I noticed a little rise in the sidewalk, so I stood on it."

Bill gave Edna an admiring smile. "That was clever as well as brave."

Moments later, Bill slid into the driver's side of the car and started the motor. Edna asked, "Why is that man so angry at you?"

"We never did get along. But I'd guess that he's probably still upset about what happened last year when I was home on leave from the army."

"What happened?"

Bill put the car in gear and turned down Pine Street. "In January of 1918, the United States Department of Justice ordered that every German alien in the country who was over the age of fourteen had to register. In Port Huron this was done at the police station. I was at the newspaper visiting my uncle when some Germans came to his office complaining about how Patrolman Greene was treating them."

"What did you do?"

"I went to the police station the next day and hung around to see what would happen. Sure enough, there was good old Wilbur giving them a hard time. He was making ethnic slurs to the men and lewd comments to the women. I told my friend Toby Sharpe how Wilbur was behaving, and he told the chief of police. Chief Chambers reprimanded Wilbur. Somehow, Wilbur figured out that I had turned him in."

Edna asked, "Why was it necessary to make the German aliens register with the government?"

"I don't think many of them posed a threat, but there were a few German terrorists in the country. There was actually a German secret service organization that planned various types of sabotage."

"Even in St. Clair County?"

Bill said, "There was a plan to blow up the St. Clair River Tunnel because war armaments were being shipped into Canada. Albert Kaltschmidt, the president of the Marine City Salt Company, was the local mastermind. The plan was to put a small cart on roller skates, fill it with dynamite, and push it into the tunnel."

"Oh, dear. Did they succeed?"

"No. A teenage girl, a German immigrant who worked for the Kaltschmidts as a maid, overheard the plot and reported it to the police. It was discovered that Albert Kaltschmidt was in charge of the German secret service in Michigan. Among other things, he was planning to organize a group of German-born citizens to invade Canada."

Edna said, "Let me get this straight. A respectable businessman, an American citizen of German descent, was a terrorist, and a German alien teenager from the working class was a heroine?"

"Right. That's why it's ridiculous to lump people into stereotypes."

"What happened to Kaltschmidt?"

"He was sentenced to four years imprisonment at Leavenworth."

Bill stopped the car in front of the Bryant home and walked Edna to the door. He said, "I'm glad you agreed to go to the movies with me."

Edna turned to face Bill, her back to the door. "I had a nice time, and a little more excitement than I anticipated."

Bill leaned forward and kissed Edna gently on the lips.

CHAPTER 30

▼

Gressley was waiting outside his apartment Thursday morning when Toby pulled up. As Gressley slid in the car, Toby said, "I'm sorry I'm a few minutes late. I overslept this morning."

"I was getting a little concerned because we need to get to Hank Peters's house as soon as possible."

"Hank Peters? Isn't he at the lumberyard?"

Gressley said, "I called the lumberyard owner last night. He said Peters was not scheduled to be at work until nine o'clock today. I want to interview him when he's not around his friends. We might get him to say something that he would be reluctant to admit if they were nearby."

Moments later, Toby parked the car in front of Hank Peters's home, a small wooden house in need of repairs. Toby said, "I think he needs to use some of the material from the lumberyard on his own house."

Gressley and Toby knocked on the front door. A small woman in a well-worn housedress opened the door. Gressley asked, "Mrs. Peters?"

"What do you want?"

Gressley introduced himself. "Patrolman Sharpe and I would like to talk to your husband."

Mrs. Peters squinted her eyes as she looked at Toby more closely. "Are you Toby? Port Huron High, class of ought six?"

Toby's eyes widened. "Sadie? Gosh, I haven't seen you in a long time. How have you been?"

Sadie Peters fumbled with a loose button on her dress as she mumbled, "OK." She moved aside so the two men could enter the dimly lit living room. She yelled, "Hank! Two police officers want to talk to you!"

Hank Peters poked his head through the kitchen doorway. "What?" His eyes blinked nervously when he saw the policemen.

Gressley said, "I have a few more questions about Saturday night." Turning to Toby, he said, "Why don't you take Mrs. Peters outside while I talk to Hank alone?"

After Toby and Sadie left, Gressley sat on the sagging sofa and studied the worn linoleum patterns on the floor.

Hank sat on a chair and began bouncing his leg. "I already told you everything I know about Saturday night. Honest."

"I just want to clarify a few things," Gressley said. "First, tell me what time you arrived at Boon Eckard's house to play poker."

"It was just a little before six. I didn't leave until about eleven."

"When did Harry Moss and Lester Johnson arrive?"

Hank tapped his fingers on his knees. "Let's see. Harry was there before me, and Lester came about ten minutes after I got there."

"And none of you left until the poker game ended?"

"That's right."

Gressley said, "I understand you and your poker buddies didn't like Russell Wilcox. Was it because of race?"

"There was more to it than that. Stockwell was always giving him special favors. Russell got pay raises while my family has to live in this flea trap. It just wasn't fair."

"Did it make you angry enough to kill him?"

Hank cringed. "Kill him? Hell, I couldn't do anything like that."

"Could Boone Eckard?"

"No ... maybe ... I don't know. But he never left the house while I was there, so he couldn't have done it."

Gressley closed his notebook and stood up. "That will be all for now." Gressley opened the front door and walked toward Toby and Sadie. "Mrs. Peters, you can go back in your house now." Sadie nodded and walked toward the house while Gressley and Toby got into the car. Toby asked, "What did you find out?"

"Hank's story was essentially the same as what he told us at the lumberyard. I have a feeling that Hank wouldn't be able to beat someone to death."

Toby started the car and headed downtown. "I think you're right about Hank. Sadie said that it just wasn't in Hank's nature to do something so violent."

Gressley asked, "How did things go yesterday at Clayton's?"

Toby said, "Clayton Boyd thinks the rope used to hang Russell is the kind you find on trapeze swings in circuses. He showed me some circus posters, and the ropes sure looked the same."

"Did you have any luck finding Mike Sweeney?"

"No. I called a total of fourteen boardinghouses and hotels. None of them had a Mike Sweeney registered. What happened at the funeral?"

Gressley said, "I got a chance to talk to Oscar Danbridge about Leroy Beckwith. Oscar said he heard that Leroy does have a girlfriend in Flint. A railroad employee named Sylvester Jackson claimed Leroy was on the train Saturday night and that they'd even had a conversation. So, I tend to put Leroy at the bottom of our suspect list, at least for the present."

"Where do you want to go now?"

"Let's stop at Farmer and Conselyea's and see if Hanton has any information for us."

Within minutes, Toby was parking in front of the shoe store. He turned to Gressley. "I'd like to talk about something else before we go inside. I have some fingerprints that I would like to send to International Association for Identification in California."

Gressley looked at Toby curiously. "Does this have anything to do with Russell's murder?"

Toby paused for a moment. When he spoke, his voice was a bare whisper. "No."

"Then why do you want it done?"

Toby tapped his fingers on the steering wheel. "A man attacked Mary on Tuesday night."

"What?"

"He came into the Majestic Theater and tried to force himself on her. Chris saw him do it."

Gressley asked, "Is Mary OK?"

"She wasn't hurt, but she's shaken up. She was afraid someone would see them together and start stories about her."

"Who attacked her?"

Toby said, "Mary thought his name was Milton Burks. But when I went to the Harrington Hotel, the clerk said his name was Benjamin Potts. He apparently left Port Huron late Tuesday night. I figured if he was using two different names, he might be some kind of criminal. If he is a crook, the IAI might have his fingerprints on record. Do you think the department would send them out?"

"Of course we'll do that. I'll talk to Chief Chambers, but I'm sure he won't object. We can also send the fingerprints to the Chicago Police Department's Bureau of Investigation. It has a large number fingerprints on many criminals throughout the Midwest. I have a friend there who would be happy to see what they have on file. Have you developed the film yet?"

"No, but I have it with me."

Gressley said, "You go on to Smith's Photography and drop off the film. He has a contract with the department to give us top priority. I'll go ahead and talk to Hanton by myself."

Toby said quietly, "Thanks, John. I really appreciate this."

$$* \quad * \quad * \quad *$$

Dave Hanton looked up and laid his cigar in an ashtray when Gressley entered the shoe store. "Ah, inspector. I have your list."

Gressley smiled. "I'm a detective, not an inspector. How many names did you find?"

Dave handed a sheet of paper to Gressley. "I was able to find eight names, dating back to April."

"I see five of them are men. Can you tell me their ages?"

Dave looked at the list and estimated each person's age. "Two are in their early thirties. The other three are about eleven, fifty, and seventy."

"I'm interested in the two who are in their early thirties. Do you know where I might find them?"

"Clarence Baxter works at the Desmond Bank and Trust. I don't know about Weldon Clark."

Gressley slipped the paper into his pocket. "Thanks, Mr. Hanton. You've been very helpful."

Dave nodded. "I read in the paper that you are in charge of the Russell Wilcox murder investigation."

Gressley said, "That's right."

"Russell was a customer of mine. I built that special shoe he wore. He was a nice person. I hope you catch the men who killed him."

Gressley shook Dave's hand. "We'll keep looking until we do."

*   *   *   *

Toby was waiting when Gressley came out of the shoe store. Gressley said, "Did you take care of the film?"

"Yes. Smith said he would give it special attention and that I can pick it up first thing tomorrow morning." Putting the car in gear, he asked, "Was Hanton able to help?"

"Maybe. He gave me the names of two men in their thirties who ordered the special heel we're looking for. One of them works at Desmond Bank and Trust. Let's go there first."

Clarence Baxter was in his office when the policemen entered the bank. Baxter's secretary asked, "May I help you?"

"We would like to talk to Mr. Baxter," Gressley said.

She looked at Toby's uniform. "This isn't about a loan, is it?"

"No. I'm Detective Gressley of the Port Huron Police Department. We have a few questions to ask your boss."

She opened the door to Mr. Baxter's office and talked to him briefly. He looked at the two police officers for a moment and then waved them into his office.

"Miss Butler said you have some questions for me. Please sit down."

Gressley sat down. Toby remained standing at the door. Gressley said, "We're investigating the murder of Russell Wilcox, and we need to follow up on some information."

Clarence Baxter's eyes widened. "What information would I have about that?"

"It's my understanding that you wear a special heel on your right shoe that leaves a distinctive mark. Is that correct?"

"Yes. But ..."

"We found that pattern at the murder scene."

Clarence groaned, "Dear God, how could that be? There must be someone else with the same kind of shoe."

"Where you were last Saturday night?"

"I was at the Gratiot Inn. The bank's board of directors sponsored a Halloween party for the staff."

Gressley asked, "What time were you there?"

"I was there at five o'clock, because my secretary and I were in charge of registration. People started to arrive at six, and a buffet was served at seven. The party lasted until about midnight."

"And you were there the whole time?"

Clarence nodded. "Yes, sir. And I was in my stupid Tom Mix cowboy outfit for every minute of it, including fake guns and some ill-fitting cowboy boots that make me look like I was bowlegged."

"Tom Mix? Did you have a lasso?"

"No. I was too busy to be carrying any kind of silly prop."

Gressley stood up and thanked Clarence for his time.

Gressley and Toby left the bank and walked to the car. Toby said, "It looks like he's got a good alibi."

"I agree. The Gratiot Inn is several miles from the lumberyard. I don't think he could have been in both places."

"Is there any possibility Miss Butler could have covered for him so he could disappear for a while? I noticed the two looked at each other in a funny way."

"I suspect the 'funny way' you saw was love."

Toby looked at Gressley, and smiled. "I suppose you're right."

Gressley asked, "What's the other name Hanton gave you?"

"Weldon Clark. Do you know him?"

Toby shook his head. "No. The name doesn't sound familiar to me."

"We need to go back to the office and check all the Clarks in the city direc-tory. But before we do, let's go to lunch and then stop by Laboys' Garage to see if Mark is there."

CHAPTER 31

▼

The Grand Trunk Railroad train ground to a stop in Oaks Corner. Sylvia Pointe grabbed her suitcase, disembarked from the train, and walked to the Hillside Inn. This was her last stop for the week, and she was beginning to feel a little fatigued. She opened the door to the inn and stepped inside.

Myrtle Terwiliger, a short, plump woman in her late forties, poked her head around the kitchen door. "Can I help you?"

"My name's Sylvia Pointe. I have a reservation for tonight."

Myrtle wiped her hands as she walked into the living room. "Goodness gracious. I didn't realize it was so late. My name is Myrtle. Would you like a cup of coffee?"

"That would be nice." Sylvia followed Myrtle into the kitchen.

As Myrtle poured the coffee, she said, "Please sit down."

"I'll stand, if you don't mind. I feel like I've been sitting all week."

Myrtle handed Sylvia the cup. "I'm excited about the meeting tonight."

Sylvia sipped some coffee. "Oh, this is good. Are you a member of the Woman's Benefit Association?"

"Goodness gracious, yes. I've been a member for nearly twenty years. When I heard Bina West speak in 1901, I signed up right away. Have you been employed at the WBA for long?"

"No. I previously worked for the Port Huron Police Department as a secretary. I wanted to be a policewoman, but decided that would never happen. When the United States got into the war with Germany, I quit the police department and joined the Red Cross Motor Corps. I just started working at the WBA in January of this year."

Myrtle asked, "Where were you assigned when you were in the Red Cross Motor Corps?"

Sylvia sat her cup down. "I was at Battle Creek for eighteen months, where we supported the soldiers at Camp Custer."

Myrtle's eyes filled with tears. "Were you there during the influenza epidemic last year?"

Sylvia saw that Myrtle was upset. She also recalled how frantic things were during the epidemic. There were nearly five thousand soldiers sick at the same time. The epidemic became so widespread in Michigan that on October 19, Governor Albert Sleeper ordered that all public places throughout Michigan be closed. For nearly a month, people were not allowed to meet in churches, theaters, pool halls, schools, or funeral homes.

Sylvia spoke quietly, "Yes, I remember those terrible times. The Red Cross provided medicines and surgical masks."

Myrtle handed Sylvia a photograph of a young soldier. "Do you recognize my son?"

"No. Was he at Camp Custer?"

Myrtle began sobbing. "Yes. He died during the influenza epidemic."

Sylvia held Myrtle in her arms. "I'm so sorry."

After a few moments, Myrtle removed herself from the embrace. She wiped her eyes. "Good Lord, what kind of hostess am I?"

Sylvia tenderly clasped Myrtle's hands. "That's alright. You take as much time as you want."

Myrtle smiled gratefully. "I'm fine now. Would you like to see your room?"

Sylvia reached down to get her suitcase. "I would like to take a little nap before tonight's meeting. Which one is mine?"

"The nicest room is on the first floor. But you can have your choice of any room you want."

Sylvia asked, "Oh, why is that?"

"Have you ever heard of the Whitecaps of America?"

"No. Is it some kind of swimming organization?"

Myrtle said, "It's a group that promotes racial hatred, and they're having a meeting at Homer Smoots's farm tomorrow night. A traveling salesman named Milton Burks was here Monday to sell uniforms to Homer. We found a pamphlet in Burks's room when we were cleaning. It said that the Whitecaps were opposed to Catholics, Jews, foreigners, and colored people. The pamphlet also indicated that Burks was not just a salesman. It turns out he's the vice president of the organization."

"It sounds a lot like the Ku Klux Klan."

Myrtle nodded. "We knew that except for you, the rest of the people who had reserved rooms for Friday night were going to that meeting. My husband was so angry after he read the pamphlet that he contacted all of them. He said there had been a misunderstanding and that the rooms had already been booked."

"That was a pretty expensive decision."

"I know, but we did it in honor of our son. He joined the army because he believed in what Woodrow Wilson said when we declared war on Germany—the world must be made safe for democracy. How can we support democracy in other countries while condoning groups like the Whitecaps who want to deny rights to people in our own country? We felt we had to do something in memory of our son."

"Your son would be proud of what you did."

Myrtle dabbed her eyes. "Can I ask you a favor?"

"Sure."

"Would you mind if I went with you to the meeting tonight?"

"I would be honored."

CHAPTER 32

▼

Luke Laboy waved to Gressley and Toby when they entered his garage. "I guess you're here to see my brother."

Mark emerged from behind the car he was working on, wiping his hands.

Gressley said, "Good afternoon. We were hoping you might be able to answer some questions about last Friday's incident near Oscar's Grocery Store."

"Luke and I were just talking about that. I think I can help, because I talked to Mike and his friend when they brought their car in for repairs. Mike Sweeney called the other man Weldon. I don't know if that was his first or last name."

"That is helpful. How old do you think Weldon is?"

Mark said, "I would guess that he's in his thirties."

"We understand Sweeney is from Port Huron," Gressley said. "Do you have any idea where Weldon is from?"

"No. I know he's not from Port Huron."

Toby asked, "Does he have any relatives here?"

"I don't think so. Sweeney mentioned something about the two of them renting a room," Mark said.

Gressley asked, "How do they know each other?"

"Both of them had been in the far west, around Montana and the Datokas. They said they worked for the Whitaker Brothers Circus."

Toby asked, "They weren't in the army?"

Mark shook his head. "I don't think so."

Gressley shook Mark's hand. "Thanks. You've been a great help."

Gressley and Toby walked to the car, and took their seats. Toby asked, "Wasn't Weldon the name you got from the shoe store?"

Gressley looked at the sheet Hanton had given him. "A Weldon Clark got the special heel just two weeks ago. I think he and Mike Sweeney have become our prime suspects."

"Do you think the Laboy brothers were in on it?"

"I doubt if Mark would have given us all that information if they were. Clark and Sweeney must have hooked up with two other people."

Toby started the car. "You're probably right. What do we do now?"

"We have about three hours before it gets dark. Let's see if we can find where Clark and Sweeney are staying. We need to check all of the houses that rent rooms."

CHAPTER 33

▼

Waking from a refreshing nap, Sylvia decided to walk to the Methodist church where her presentation would be held that night. She entered the church and approached a tall, bald man near the front. She said, "Excuse me. My name is Sylvia Pointe and I'll be conducting a meeting sponsored by the Woman's Benefit Association tonight."

The man extended his hand. "Pleased to meet you. I'm Reverend Tom Rossman. I decided to straighten things up for tonight. How many women do you think will attend?"

"The local chapter thought there would be about fifty. May I use the pulpit?"

"Of course. My wife is really looking forward to your presentation. She's anxious to start voting in the national elections next year."

"That's great." Sylvia spent a few minutes walking around the church. She shook Reverend Rossman's hand again and said, "Everything looks fine. I'm looking forward to meeting your wife and the other women tonight."

When Sylvia returned to the Hillside Inn, she waved to Earl Terwiliger who was raking leaves that had fallen from the large oak tree in the front yard. She entered the inn and walked to the kitchen. "That smells wonderful. What are we having for dinner?" she asked.

Myrtle Terwiliger answered. "Roast chicken, sweet potatoes, peas, and freshly baked bread."

"I can't wait. I had an early lunch so I could catch the train. I'm famished."

"Is five o'clock OK? I know the meeting starts at seven, and I assume you would like a little time between the meal and the meeting."

"That would be perfect. If you don't mind, I'd like to place a call to Port Huron before dinner."

"Sure. The phone is in the living room."

Sylvia picked up the receiver and gave the operator John Gressley's number. Moments later, John answered.

"Hi, John. I made it to the Hillside Inn in Oaks Corner."

"It's great to hear your voice. How's your trip going?"

"It's been exciting. The women are eager to learn all they can about voting in their first national election. How's the murder investigation?"

"We have two main suspects—Mike Sweeney and Weldon Clark. But we have two major problems. We can't find them, and we have no idea who their accomplices were. We think they're renting a room somewhere in the city. Toby and I spent three hours canvassing all the houses north of the Black River."

"Oh my. You must be very tired."

John grunted. "My feet certainly are. I'm soaking them in Epsom Salts right now."

Sylvia asked, "Do you think you're going to be able to make it tomorrow night?"

"I don't know. I feel like we might really be close to breaking the case. I'll call you tomorrow to let you know."

"I understand. Is there any other news?"

John said, "Toby and Mary had a situation. A man tried to sexually molest Mary on Tuesday night."

"That's horrid! Who would do anything like that?"

"It was some stranger to Port Huron. He's a traveling salesman by the name of Milton Burks."

Sylvia gasped. "Milton Burks?"

"Yes. Don't tell me you know him."

"He stayed here at the Hillside Inn earlier this week. He was selling uniforms to a racist group called the Whitecaps of America. He's also the organization's vice president."

John asked, "Is that the meeting that's going to be on a farm near Oaks Corner?"

"You've heard about the meeting?"

"Someone put a flyer up in the office a couple of weeks ago." He paused for a moment before saying, "Why don't you come home tomorrow when you're done? Groups like that are upset about women getting the right to vote. You might find yourself in an uncomfortable situation if any of them find out why you are in Oaks Corner."

"I'm staying here, darling. And I hope you can make it tomorrow night. I bought a negligee in Flint that's both naughty and nice."

After they had said their good-byes, Sylvia hung up the receiver and turned to walk to the kitchen. She had only taken a few steps when the phone rang.

Myrtle yelled, "Sylvia, could you answer that? I'm busy with the chicken right now."

Sylvia picked up the receiver. "Hillside Inn."

The operator said, "I have a long-distance call from Port Huron."

Sylvia, thinking John might have thought of something else he needed to tell her, said, "Hi."

The voice was not John's. "Good evening. I was wondering if you have a room available for tomorrow night."

"I'm not sure. Could you wait for a moment? I'll get one of the owners. Could you tell me your name?"

"Bill Boyd."

Sylvia laughed. "Are you kidding me? This is Sylvia Pointe."

"Sylvia! I heard you were working for the Woman's Benefit Association and that you would be speaking in Oaks Corner tonight. But I didn't know you were staying at the Hillside Inn."

"There aren't very many other places in Oaks Corner. Why do you want a room?"

"I decided to attend the Whitecaps of America meeting tomorrow night. I thought it might make an interesting story."

"Won't they get angry if they know a newspaper reporter's there?"

"When I called the organizer, a Mr. Smoots, I just told him I was interested in coming. He said they had several uniforms left, so I'll be in a disguise. I figure it will be like going to a Halloween party," Bill said.

"Hold on for a minute. I'll see what Myrtle has to say about you staying here."

After talking to Mrs. Terwiliger, Sylvia returned the phone. "She said it was alright. But watch yourself. You know how you get into trouble."

"I believe you're talking rot, my dear Sylvia. But, I promise to be careful. I should be there by about four o'clock."

*   *   *   *

Homer Smoots and his son Warren were breathing heavily and sweating profusely as they admired the large cross they had just erected.

Homer said, "I think that will do the job."

"Do you think those ropes will hold the cross together when we set it on fire tomorrow night?"

Homer wiped his forehead with a large red bandana. "I'm sure they will."

Warren asked, "What else needs to be done?"

"Tomorrow afternoon, we'll tie the rags around the cross and set up the old wagon for the speakers to stand on."

"How many are comin'?"

"Nearly three hundred."

Warren rubbed his hands on the cross. "I'm goin' to miss this old oak tree."

Homer put his hand on his son's shoulder. Speaking in a hushed voice, he said, "It's going to be used for a much grander purpose."

CHAPTER 34

▼

The first thing Gressley did when he arrived at work Friday morning was to knock on Chief Chambers' office door. Chambers motioned him in. "I thought I might bring you up to date on the murder investigation," Gressley said.

"Is anyone in jail yet?"

"No, but I think we're getting closer. Toby and I think the rope used to hang Russell Wilcox is the same type that's used for trapeze swings, and we have the names of two people who are apparently linked with the Whitaker Brothers Circus.

"Whitaker Brothers? I've never heard of it."

"Apparently it's a small circus out west. Clayton Boyd is something of an expert on circuses. We're going to talk to him again this morning to see if he can give us any additional information. I believe two of the suspects, Mike Sweeney and Weldon Clark, are staying at a rented room somewhere in town. We're going to continue looking for them after we talk to Mr. Boyd."

"Do you need any help? I could talk to Sergeant Williams to see if anyone's free."

"That would be great. We could use some help this afternoon if we don't have any luck this morning." Gressley paused for a moment. "There's something else I want to talk about."

Chambers raised his eyebrows, "What?"

Gressley placed the packet of photographs on the table. "A man by the name of Milton Burks tried to sexually molest Mary Sharpe the other night."

"Good Lord. Is she all right?"

"She wasn't physically hurt, but the whole thing has been unsettling. Toby found out that Burks was a traveling salesman staying at the Harrington Hotel under the name of Benjamin Potts. Toby went to the hotel and took these pictures of recent fingerprints. He figured that since the attacker was using an alias, he might be wanted by the police in other cities. If so, his fingerprints might be on record. I want to send these fingerprints to the IAI in California and the Chicago Police Department's Bureau of Identification to see if they can help."

"By all means. I'll have them sent out this morning."

"Thank you, Chief." John stood up. "Just one more thing."

"Yes?"

"Have you decided who to promote to sergeant?"

Chambers shook his head. "I haven't made a final decision."

"Please give serious thought to Toby. He's done an excellent job on this murder investigation, and I don't think he has a serious drinking problem."

"Sergeant Williams came in yesterday to tell me the same thing. He said that Wilbur Greene had been exaggerating about Toby's drinking. Right now, Toby's at the top of my list."

*   *   *   *

Clayton Boyd was finishing a walk when he saw two familiar police officers standing in front of his house. He shouted, "I'll be there in a minute!"

Toby jogged over to Clayton. "Good to see you're out exercising."

Clayton said, "It's part of Dr. Nelson's fitness program. I walk at a moderate rate for a mile in the morning, and another mile in the afternoon. Am I correct in assuming that this is not a social visit?"

"You're right. We have some more questions about circuses."

Reaching the house, Clayton opened the door and followed the policemen inside. He said, "Go on into my study."

Once they were seated, Clayton asked, "How can I help the police today?"

Gressley said, "First, I want to thank you for your suggestion about the rope."

Clayton smiled brightly. "You're welcome."

Gressley continued. "Also, Toby thought you might be able to give us some information about the Whitaker Brothers Circus. Have you ever heard of it?"

"Yes. It's a small circus out west. It tours Montana, the Dakotas, and Wyoming during the summer. It also goes into the Canadian provinces of Alberta and Saskatchewan. Its employees take October, November, and December off before touring Arizona, New Mexico, and California during the winter months."

Toby asked, "So the employees would not be with the circus right now?"

"That's correct."

Gressley asked, "Do you have an address for the owners? I want to see if I can get a list of their employees."

"I'm sorry, but I don't know their address."

As the policemen began to leave, Clayton asked, "Did you hear what happened to Bill last night?"

Toby said, "I understand he had a date. Did it go OK?"

"The date went fine, but he was ambushed by that scoundrel Wilbur Greene. He and Edna were walking to his car when Greene came up and pushed Bill into the street and then insulted Edna. Bill was acting like a raging bull when he came home."

Gressley asked, "Did he report it?"

"No. He wanted to talk to either you or Toby, and he knew you were busy with the murder investigation today."

Toby asked, "Was Greene with anyone?"

Clayton thought for a moment. "Bill didn't catch his last name, but his first name was Clyde."

Gressley asked, "Is Bill at the newspaper? We could stop by and get a formal statement."

"I'm afraid not. He's got an interview with some people at the Wills Sainte Claire Motor Car Company in Marysville this morning. Then he's headed for Oaks Corner to attend the Whitecaps of America rally tonight."

Gressley's face blanched. "Oaks Corner?"

Clayton said, "Yes. He called the Hillside Inn last night and reserved a room for this evening. He promised to be very careful."

His voiced strained, Gressley managed to said, "Sylvia Pointe is staying at the same inn."

Clayton put his face in the hands. He muttered, "Jehovah of Hosts. That's not good news. Who knows what will happen when those two get together?"

Gressley walked quickly out of the house. Attempting to reassure Clayton, Toby said, "Don't worry, Mr. Boyd. I'm sure they won't get into trouble." As Toby ran to catch up with Gressley, he shouted, "Thanks for the information about the circus."

Outside, Gressley banged the top of the car with his fist.

Toby stood beside Gressley and asked, "What are you going to do about Oaks Corner?"

Gressley struggled to regain his composure. "Sylvia's busy with meetings this morning, so I can't call her now. I'll try this afternoon. For now, let's see if we can find Mike Sweeney and Weldon Clark."

＊   ＊   ＊   ＊

Gressley and Toby spent the remainder of the morning trying to find out where the two suspects were staying. Frustrated by their lack of success, they slumped into two chairs at the Fisherman's Restaurant. After ordering sandwiches and coffee, the two sat quietly for a few minutes.

Finally, Gressley said, "I didn't realize so many people rented rooms."

"I think it's because there's a housing shortage right now."

"Chambers said he would see who's available to help us this afternoon."

"It's nearly one o'clock," Toby said. "Let's work for another hour before we go back to the office."

Gressley finished his meal and pushed his plate to the side. "That's fine with me. I'm going to call the Hillside Inn to see if Sylvia's back from her meeting."

Moments later, he returned. "Nobody answered. I'll try to call her again late this afternoon."

"Do you really think she and Bill will get into trouble?"

Gressley said. "I hope not. But they both can be pretty opinionated, and neither one is likely to back down from a confrontation."

＊   ＊   ＊   ＊

Toby parked the car on Court Street. He pointed to the third house from the corner. "There's a 'room for rent' sign over there. The two men got out of the car. Gressley had become so tired of introducing himself and Toby, that he'd asked that the two start taking turns. It was now his turn.

A middle-aged woman answered the door. "Yes?"

"My name is Detective Gressley, and this is Patrolman Sharpe. We're looking for two men—Mike Sweeney and Weldon Clark. Are they renting a room from you?"

"I'm Mrs. Mitchell. The two men you're looking for have been staying here for about three weeks."

Gressley's eyes widened. "Are they in?"

"No, they left this morning. They didn't say where they were going."

Toby said, "Mike Sweeney has family in Port Huron. Do you know why he would be renting a room instead of staying with his family?"

Mrs. Mitchell looked down the street before saying, "Maybe we could talk inside."

Once they were seated in the living room, Mrs. Mitchell said, "Mike and his dad had a falling out two years ago. Mike was twenty-one at the time and didn't want to go into the army. He went to Canada to avoid the draft. His dad called him a coward and said he never wanted to see him again."

Toby asked, "Then why is he in town?"

"He's here to see his mother. She visits him here about every other day. Her husband doesn't know anything about it."

Gressley said, "We understand that he might have some kind of association with a circus. Can you tell us anything about that?"

"According to Mrs. Sweeney, her son joined the circus last year when it on location in Canada. He got a job as a clown. When the circus came back to the states, he was able to get across the border without any problems. Of course, now that the war's over the government isn't looking for him anymore."

Toby asked, "But his dad still won't have anything to do with him?"

Mrs. Mitchell nodded. "Sad, but true."

Gressley asked, "Do you know anything about Weldon Clark?"

"Not much. I know he worked for the circus in some capacity, but I'm not sure what. He's real quiet and keeps to himself."

Toby asked, "Does anyone else come here, besides Mike's mother?"

"Clyde Miller and some mean man with a face like a weasel." She looked down at her hands. "I think I heard Mike say that he was a policeman."

Gressley and Toby looked at each other in astonishment. Toby asked, "Wilbur Greene?"

Mrs. Mitchell said, "Yes, that's the name. I didn't like him one iota."

Gressley asked, "What do you know about Clyde Miller?"

"Not much. He seems nice enough when Wilbur's not around. Only heaven know why he wants to be around someone like Wilbur."

"Can you give us a description?" asked Toby.

"He's about five feet, nine inches tall and skinny. He's got blond hair and freckles."

The policemen stood up. Gressley said, "Thank you, Mrs. Mitchell. You have been very helpful."

CHAPTER 35

▼

Sylvia Pointe was relaxing in the living room of the Hillside Inn, chatting with Earl Terwiliger, when Bill strolled in and introduced himself. "I have reserved a room for the night."

Earl rose from his chair. "Yes sir, Mr. Boyd. You will be in room number two. It's on the main floor right next to Sylvia's."

Bill sat his suitcase down and took a seat. "Please call me Bill." He turned to Sylvia. "You don't snore too loudly, do you?"

Sylvia snorted. "The walls are thick. You won't hear me if I do."

Earl said, "I understand you have known each other for a long time."

"We met in 1911 when I started working for my uncle at the *Port Huron Star.* Sylvia's been my main source of information at the police department ever since."

Sylvia laughed. "That's because no one else at the department will talk to him."

Bill glanced at Earl and grimaced. He said, "Now don't you believe anything she says. My best friend is Patrolman Tobias Sharpe."

Sylvia said, "Well, maybe Toby will talk to you sometimes."

Earl grinned. "If I didn't know any better, I would think you were brother and sister the way you tease. Sylvia was telling me you taught her how to drive."

"Holy Moses, that was a frightening experience."

"Bill owned a car made in Port Huron by the Havers Motor Car Company. It was a two-passenger speedster. I had this idea that if I learned how to drive, the police department might let me be a policewoman. But it didn't work out."

Bill became serious. "It was the police department's loss. Sylvia would make a terrific policewoman."

Sylvia asked, "What kind of fancy car do you have now?"

"A 1917 Cadillac. I still got a two-passenger car, but this one also has a rumble seat. The car rides like a dream."

Earl asked, "Aren't you the reporter who helped expose the kidnapping ring in Port Huron a few years ago?"

"That's right. We were able to drive Velvet Cushion and her gang out of business."

"Do you have any idea what happened to Velvet?" asked Earl.

"Not really. But I've fantasized that she gained seventy pounds and became a sheep farmer in Montana."

"That would be an interesting conclusion to her life," Earl said. "I understand you're going to the Whitecaps of America rally. What time do you plan to go?"

"I want to go around six, because I have to buy a uniform and I would like to have a mask on before many people get there. I don't want to be recognized."

Earl rubbed his hands together. "Do you mind if I go with you? I'm kind of interested in hearing what they have to say."

Sylvia asked, "Won't that be a problem? Some of those people might be angry at you for canceling their reservations."

"I was thinking we could take my truck," said Earl. "All Ford trucks look the same, so I doubt if anyone would recognize it in the dark. I would stay in the truck until you bought me a uniform. That way nobody would see my face."

"That's fine with me. I would enjoy the company. Plus, you can give me directions on how to find the farm."

"What about me?" asked Sylvia. "I'd love to see what you men do at those meetings."

Bill laughed nervously. "Now, don't be foolish. Only heaven knows what would happen if they caught a woman spying on them."

"I can just sit in the car. Nobody would even know I was there."

Earl leaned over and touched Sylvia's hand. "I really don't think that would be a good idea."

Sylvia narrowed her eyes, and glared at the two men. Bill had seen this look on earlier occasions, and had dubbed it the "Sylvia Stare." He tried to avoid it as much as possible.

CHAPTER 36

▼

Oscar Danbridge was restocking the condiments section when he noticed a white man enter his grocery store. He watched as the man approached him.

"Mr. Danbridge?"

"Yes."

"I'm Luke Laboy, and I'd like to talk to you for a minute."

Oscar gripped the neck of a catsup bottle. "I know who you are. What do you want to talk about?"

"I want to apologize for harassing Russell Wilcox in front of your store last Friday. It was a stupid thing to do, and I'm sorry."

"Are you saying you didn't have anything to do with his death?"

Luke shook his head. "I swear on a stack of Bibles that my brother and I were working at our garage."

"What about the man who got out of the car and wanted to chase Russell?"

"Mike Sweeney? I don't know why he did that. I remember Mike used to make fun of Russell when we were in high school."

Oscar asked, "You knew Russell?"

"Yes, and I'm ashamed to say that I joined in the teasing. But I'd like to think I've grown up since then."

"The person you ought to apologize to is his mother."

Luke said, "I don't know where she lives."

Oscar relaxed his grip on the bottle and returned it to the shelf. "She's at Stockwell's lumberyard. Mr. Stockwell wanted to talk to her about some kind of memorial to Russell."

"I wouldn't know what to say."

"Tell her the same thing you told me. I'll go with you."

Luke nodded. "I'd appreciate that."

*   *   *   *

Mabel looked up from her desk as Gressley and Toby rushed into the police station.

Gressley asked, "Do you have Wilbur Greene's schedule?"

Mabel said, "He's not working this weekend. He requested today, tomorrow, and Sunday off."

Sergeant Williams overheard the conversation and walked over to Mabel's desk. "Why are you asking about Wilbur?"

Toby said, "We just found out he's been associating with our two main suspects in the Russell Wilcox murder—Mike Sweeney and Weldon Clark."

Williams's eyes widened. "Do you think Wilbur might be involved?"

Gressley said, "At the very least he might know something that would be helpful."

Williams scratched his head. "You know, Wilbur was the one who arrested Russell for stealing that car last summer. He was really angry when Russell was released. He was absolutely convinced that Russell was guilty."

Toby said, "We all know how Wilbur can hold a grudge. Maybe he decided to take it upon himself to punish Russell."

Gressley turned to Mabel. "Do you have Wilbur's address?"

Mabel wrote down the address and handed it to Gressley. "Here it is, but I doubt you'll find him there."

"Why?"

"I heard him saying he was going out of town."

Gressley asked, "Did he say where he was headed?"

Mabel thought for a moment. "No, but I got a pretty good idea. Wilbur didn't know it, but I saw him sneak in here and post that flyer about the White-caps of America. I think he might be going to that meeting tonight."

Gressley rushed to the door. "Let's hurry. Maybe we can still catch him before he leaves."

*   *   *   *

Richard Stockwell smiled when Freeda Wilcox knocked on his office at the lumberyard. "I'm glad you were able to come today. Please sit down."

Freeda said, "Thank you for attending Russell's funeral."

"You're welcome. Russell was a fine young man. As I told you on the phone, my wife and I would like to make a memorial in Russell's name."

"What do you have in mind?"

Richard said, "We would like to create an annual Russell Wilcox scholarship at the Port Huron Business College. Would that be OK with you?"

Freeda felt tears on her cheeks. She wiped her eyes before speaking. "That would be wonderful. Did you know that Lillie Mae Grant told Russell that she wanted to attend the business college? She's interested in becoming a bookkeeper."

"Then I think she should be the recipient of the first scholarship. Winter classes begin in January. Would she want to start then?"

"I'm sure she would."

"We might have a job for her when she completes the program."

Freeda stood up. "Thank you for doing this in Russell's memory. God bless you."

"It's the least we could do," Stockwell said.

They were leaving his office when Oscar Danbridge and Luke Laboy came striding toward them. Oscar said, "Freeda, this young man has something he wants to tell you."

Freeda looked at Luke quizzically.

Luke ran his hand through his hair. "I would like to talk about your son for a few minutes."

Oscar said, "I think the two of you need to be alone." He turned Stockwell. "Can they use your office for a few minutes?"

"Certainly. Take as much time as you need."

CHAPTER 37

▼

Sylvia Pointe was unusually quiet during the evening meal at the Hillside Inn. When Myrtle Terwiliger got up to serve mince pie and coffee, Sylvia excused herself.

Earl asked, "Anything wrong with your friend?"

Bill said, "She might be upset because we told her she couldn't come with us tonight."

When Bill and Earl finished their dessert and coffee, they walked into the living room to get their jackets. Earl looked puzzled. He turned to his wife and asked, "Have you see my Mackinaw jacket?"

Myrtle quickly glanced outside, then looked at Earl. "It's in the sewing room. I need to replace a button that came off." She picked up a denim jacket. "Wear this tonight."

Earl put on the jacket and kissed Myrtle. "We should be back by nine o'clock."

Myrtle held her husband tightly and whispered, "Please be careful."

Earl kissed her on the forehead. "I will."

Once outside, Bill and Earl walked toward the Ford truck. Earl opened the driver's door and sprang back in surprise. Sylvia, dressed in overalls and Earl's Mackinaw jacket, was sitting behind the wheel. She said, "I've decided to go with you tonight."

Bill peered in from the passenger's side. "Are you out of your mind? We can't let you go."

Sylvia said, "I don't think you have a choice."

Bill said, "Earl and I can take my car."

Sylvia grinned. "I removed the spark plugs and hid them. So you'll have to drag me from the truck kicking and screaming, or let me go along."

Bill moaned and turned to Earl. "What do you think?"

Earl asked, "Do you promise to stay in the truck?"

"Yes. Bill can bring me a uniform." She pulled a ten-dollar bill from a pocket in the Mackinaw jacket. "Here's the money."

Earl looked at Bill. "Well, I guess we don't have any choice."

Sylvia shifted to the middle of the seat so Earl and Bill could get in.

Earl started the engine. "Did my wife help you with your outfit?"

Sylvia nodded. "Don't be angry with her. I practically forced her to give me a pair of your overalls and a jacket."

They rode for a few minutes before Sylvia asked, "How far is it to Smoots's farm?"

"We've gone nearly a mile. It's about two miles further."

Bill said, "Do either of you know how to put the spark plugs back into my car?"

Sylvia smiled. "You don't have to. I never took them out."

Earl looked on curiously as Bill laughed heartily.

CHAPTER 38

▼

Gressley opened the car door before the vehicle had come to a complete stop. He ran to the house where Wilbur Greene rented an apartment and began banging loudly on the door. A little white-haired woman opened the door. "Land of Goshen, what's all this noise about?"

"I'm Detective Gressley of the police department. Is Wilbur home?"

"No. Some men picked him up about an hour ago."

"Do you know where he was going?"

The woman thought for a moment. "I heard him say something about Oaks Corner."

"Do you have a phone?"

"Yes."

Gressley stepped into the house, accidentally brushing against the woman. "I need to use it for an emergency."

"You don't have to be so darn pushy. It's in the living room."

Gressley rushed to the phone and rang the operator.

When the operator answered, Gressley shouted, "I want to place a long-distance call to the Hillside Inn at Oaks Corner."

On the third ring, Gressley heard a voice say, "Hillside Inn."

"Is Sylvia Pointe there?"

"No. She left about ten minutes ago."

"Where did she go?"

"With whom am I speaking?"

"I'm Detective Gressley of the Port Huron Police Department. I'm concerned that Sylvia is in trouble. Now please tell me where she is!"

"She went to the Whitecaps of America rally with my husband and Bill Boyd."

Gressley's face flushed scarlet as he slammed the receiver down. He ran outside where Toby was waiting and yelled, "Get in the car! We're going to Oaks Corner."

Within minutes, Toby and Gressley were headed south on Military Street. Toby asked, "Do you think this is a good idea? We don't have any jurisdiction in Oaks Corner."

"I've got to make sure Sylvia's safe. If Wilbur Greene sees Bill there could be trouble, and Sylvia would be right in the middle of a real mess."

They drove for a few minutes before Toby slapped his hand on the steering wheel. "Jeez, I forgot about Amanda's play."

"I'm afraid you're going to miss it."

"Can I at least let them know I won't be there? Mary will be worried if I don't call her. It'll only take a couple of minutes."

"Stockwell's lumberyard is only a few blocks from here. We can stop there."

Richard Stockwell, Luke Laboy, and Oscar Danbridge were standing in the lumberyard parking lot when Toby screeched to a stop and jumped out of his car. Toby asked, "Can I use your phone? It's an emergency!"

"Certainly. It's in my office."

Toby ran to the office and rang his home phone number. He tapped his fingers impatiently on Mr. Stockwell's desk. *Come on, Mary. Please answer.*

"Hello."

"Mary. I won't be able to go to the play tonight. Gressley and I are going to Oaks Corner. It has to do with the murder case."

"You have to go tonight?"

"It's a long story, but we think we know who the murderers are, and Gressley's afraid that Sylvia might be in danger."

"Oh, dear. Amanda will be really disappointed, but I'll try to explain it to her."

"Tell her I promise I'll go tomorrow night. And tell her that thing you say to actors to wish them luck."

Mary asked, "Do you mean 'break a leg?'"

"Yeah. Tell her to break a leg. Are you going to feel safe going back to the Majestic Theater?"

"I'm sure Milton Burks is gone. Besides, I'll be sitting next to friends and relatives. Please be careful in Oaks Corner."

"I will."

Toby hurried back to the car, where Gressley was standing with Luke and Oscar who were holding hunting rifles. Gressley had binoculars. Gressley said, "I guess we're going to have some company. They convinced me it might be a good idea if they came along. Richard gave them his guns."

Luke said, "It might even up the odds if Wilbur is there with Mike, Weldon, and Clyde."

Toby glanced at Gressley and thought, *Oh, boy. What are we getting into?*

CHAPTER 39

▼

Earl Terwiliger parked his truck about one hundred feet from a large farm wagon. The wagon was located in what had been a cornfield earlier in the year. Stretched across the wagon, and supported by poles, was a single strand of lights. Several feet to the right of the wagon was a huge cross wrapped with rags.

Several people, dressed in white robes and masks, were strolling about the field. The three men standing near the wagon were not wearing masks. Earl pointed toward the three men. "Those are the organizers of tonight's shindig."

Sylvia asked, "Why don't they have masks?"

Earl shrugged his shoulders. "I don't know. Maybe they think everyone already knows them."

Bill asked, "Who are they?"

"Homer Smoots is the one in pale blue. The Reverend Bobby Maddox is in red, and Buck Taylor is in black."

Sylvia said, "I think somebody's got a weird sense of humor."

"Why?" asked Bill.

"Are you familiar with the *Four Horsemen of the Apocalypse?*"

"Yes, I just finished Ibanez's book."

"What are the colors used to represent the four horsemen?"

Bill thought for a moment. "By Jove! White is for pestilence, red for war, black for famine, and the pale horseman is death."

All three fell silent. Finally, Bill spoke in a somber voice. "I better go buy our uniforms before more people arrive."

Bill got out of the truck and walked toward the wagon where Buck Taylor was standing. "Excuse me, do you have any uniforms for sale?"

"We have a few left. What's your name?"

"Gary Blake. I want to buy three."

"Three?"

"Yes. The other two are for my friends Dave and Gordon."

"Why can't they get their own uniforms?"

"Gordon's over there in those trees. He had to relieve himself before the rally. Dave's staying in the truck because he has a broken leg."

Buck looked in the direction of the woods. "I don't see nobody. He should have used the two-seater outhouse."

Bill smiled. "That's probably where he's at. How much do I owe you?"

"That will be thirty dollars."

Bill paid for the uniforms and tucked them under his arm. He turned away from the makeshift stage and walked quickly to the truck where his fellow actors were anxiously waiting.

CHAPTER 40

▼

Nearly three hundred men dressed in white robes, with their faces hidden behind masks, milled about the wagon at Homer Smoots's farm. Their murmuring voices resembled the buzzing of a swarm of wasps. They quieted when Homer leaped onto the wagon and introduced himself.

"I want to welcome all of you patriots to tonight's meeting of the Whitecaps of America. We are here because we are true-blue Americans who seek to uphold the Constitution of the United States.

"The Whitecaps are opposed to labor unions, Communists, and any others who attempt to undermine our great country. I encourage you to support U. S. Justice Department's effort to find all of the people who want to subvert our government. It has two hundred thousand names of suspects, and the list is still growing.

"During the war, the Liberty Loan Committees in many Michigan counties kept records on the people who refused to buy their fair share of war bonds. I propose we assist the Justice Department's effort by encouraging our state and local governments to make these names available to the public. These disloyal, so-called Americans must be identified and punished."

Several people in the audience yelled, "Hang 'em!"

Homer raised his hands. "Now, of course, all of this should be done without violence. Milton Burks, vice president of the Whitecaps, told me personally that we should only use violence when necessary."

Bill leaned closer to Earl Terwiliger and whispered, "Smoots sounds like a budding politician to me."

"He's planning to run for the state senate next year," Earl said.

Homer continued from his stage. "Let's give a warm welcome for our main speaker, the Reverend Bobby Maddox of the Church of Zealous Righteousness." A wild cheer erupted as Reverend Maddox, adorned in his red uniform, climbed onto the wagon.

$$* \qquad * \qquad * \qquad *$$

Nervous laughter could be heard backstage at the Majestic Theater as the actors waited for the first act of *Two Families—One America*. Miss Sibella gathered the cast into a circle. She said, "Everyone has worked hard the past several weeks. I'm proud of what you have done, and I'm sure the play will be a success. Through this play, we will be able to show people that America's true goal is to respect all individuals, regardless of race or national background."

Clara looked at the actors. "Just one more thing. What have I been teaching you to mind when you are on stage?"

Amanda Sharpe said, "We're to mind our p's and a's."

"That's right. Now I want you to all hold hands and say, 'mind our p's and a's.'"

$$* \qquad * \qquad * \qquad *$$

The Reverend Bobby Maddox, his crisp, rapid-fire cadence puncturing the autumn air like a machine gun, shouted, "Homer Smoots highlighted the political aspects of the Whitecaps of America. I want to remind you that the Whitecaps are also opposed to Jews, Catholics, foreign-born trash, and Nigras. The only true Americans are native-born, white Protestants.

"Ephesians 6:5 says 'slaves, obey your earthly masters with fear and trembling.' The decline of the United States began when we disobeyed God's will and ended slavery. Now black men want to have our white women. We won't let that happen. And trust me when I say that God is unhappy about this trend toward tolerance. Last year's influenza epidemic was a sign of his wrath."

Maddox paused for a moment before saying, "And we all know what the Jews want."

Someone shouted, "Our money."

Reverend Maddox grinned. "That's true. But they want more than just our money. What they really want is revealed in a frightening document called *The Protocols of the Learned Elders of Zion*. They want to use their money to undermine the government of the United States."

He surveyed the audience. "And make no mistake, my friends. The Catholics also want to take over our country. They are storing up guns in the sewers at Notre Dame University as well as many other places around the United States. When the pope gives the word, Catholics will rise up in armed rebellion.

"Of all the Catholic foreigners, the wops from Italy are the worse. They think their Italian culture is superior, and they refuse to learn to speak English. They are dark skinned, uneducated, and have a criminal nature. Italians should not be allowed into the country."

*   *   *   *

As the second act of *Two Families—One America* was about to end, Rosa Campanella stood in the center of the Majestic Theater's stage crying.

Amanda entered stage right. "Dear friend, why are you crying?"

"Some boys chased me home from school, making fun of me."

Amanda held Rosa's hand. "Why did they do that?"

"They called me names. Terrible names just because I'm Italian. Why do people have to be so mean to each other?"

Still holding Rosa's hand, Amanda turned to face the audience. She tilted her chin to be able to project her voice to the balcony. With perfect articulation, she said, "I believe we should live by the Golden Rule. 'Do unto others as you would have them do unto you.'"

Amanda and Rosa stood basking in warm applause as the curtain fell to end act two.

*   *   *   *

The blood red sleeves of Reverend Maddox's robe fluttered as his arms flailed. "The ravages of the Great War and the influenza pandemic are signs that Armageddon is near. Be on the lookout, my fellow Americans, because Satan now walks among us. We are told that the Antichrist will be rich and popular. And who is richer and more popular in the world today than Herbert Hoover?

"Hoover became popular when he was director of the European Relief and Reconstruction Committee. He is so popular in the United States right now that both the Republican and Democratic parties want him to be their candidate for president.

"The numbers tell us that Herbert Hoover must be the Prince of Darkness. H is the eighth letter of the alphabet. Eight times eight is sixty-four. Multiply sixty-four times ten and you get six hundred forty. When you add the twenty six letters of the alphabet, the number becomes six—six—six."

Caught up in his numerical revelation, Reverend Maddox did not notice the skeptical look that appeared on Homer's face.

Maddox continued. "Hoover says he does not aspire to be president of the United States. Do not be fooled. He wants that position badly, and if he gets it, you need to be prepared for Armageddon."

Bill felt lucky he was wearing a mask, because he was unable to suppress a smile. He regarded Reverend Maddox' speech as one of the most ridiculous he had ever heard. Bill wondered how many in the audience actually believed what they were hearing.

*   *   *   *

Amanda Sharpe and the rest of the cast bowed as the audience applauded enthusiastically. When the applause ended, Amanda ran to meet her family. She yelled, "Did you like it?"

Mary held Amanda in her arms. "We loved it."

Chris poked Amanda on the shoulder. "You were really good."

Amanda's grandparents smiled proudly. Her grandmother said, "Your play had a truly Christian message of how we should treat our neighbors with respect."

CHAPTER 41

▼

As the car from Port Huron approached the Smoots field, Gressley said, "This is close enough."

Toby parted the car about one-half mile from the Whitecaps rally. He said, "Look at all the people. What are they doing?

Gressley looked through the binoculars. "There are several hundred people in white robes watching two men on a makeshift stage. Someone in black is standing beside a large cross, holding a torch."

*   *   *   *

Homer Smoots was perplexed by the mathematical formula he has just heard recited. Up until a few minutes ago, Homer had considered Herbert Hoover one of America's greatest heroes. Now he didn't know what to think.

Homer spoke hesitantly, "Ah … thank you Reverend Maddox for that … ah … interesting … ah … idea. We will now conclude our rally. After Buck Taylor, our sergeant of arms, sets the cross on fire we will all sing 'The Old Rugged Cross.'"

Buck ceremoniously placed his torch on the kerosene-soaked rags. He jumped when the fire blazed stronger than he'd expected. The intense heat caused some of the men standing closest to the cross to involuntarily move backward. As people retreated from the fire, someone accidentally stepped on Bill's foot.

Bill said, "That's OK, my dear fellow. I only walk on the bottoms."

Another man growled. "I recognize that voice."

Before Bill knew what was happening, Wilbur Greene had grabbed Bill's mask and ripped it from his face. "I knew it." Pointing his finger at Bill, Wilbur screamed, "That's Bill Boyd. He's a nigger-lovin' Jew-lovin' Communist."

Some of the men turned and moved menacingly toward Bill.

Bill raised his hands. "That's a lie. I'm not a Communist. How could I be a Communist and also support a newspaper that tries to make a profit? Isn't that what capitalism is all about? I think he meant to say that I am a columnist."

Wilbur jerked at Bill's arm. "Ignore this idiot's blather. Let's teach him a lesson."

Before anyone could respond, a truck's motor roared, and a set of headlights flashed through the darkness. Bill yelled, "Everybody get back, there's a madman at the wheel of that truck!"

The crowd that had surrounded Bill and Earl immediately moved out of the way of the careening vehicle. Sylvia slid to a stop and yelled, "Jump in!"

Bill and Earl leaped into the bed of the truck as Sylvia sped away spewing gravel on the surprised Whitecaps.

Wilbur, seething with anger, yelled, "Let's get them."

Nearly thirty people ran to their cars and trucks with the intention of following Sylvia. The rest stood in silence. A few ripped off their robes and threw them on the ground before walking away. Homer Smoots, stunned by the rapidly deteriorating situation, sat dejectedly on the wagon.

✳   ✳   ✳   ✳

Toby pointed toward the Smoots's farm. "Oh, my God. Look at that cross. It's lighting up the entire sky."

Gressley, still looking through the binoculars, said, "Something strange just happened. Two people jumped in a truck, and it's coming this way. Now there are about ten cars and trucks following it."

Luke picked up a rifle. "The people in the truck might need our help."

Oscar whispered, "Dear Lord, forgive us for our sins."

✳   ✳   ✳   ✳

Bill lifted his head and shouted, "Thanks for the ride."

Sylvia yelled back, "Keep your fool head down. They might have guns."

No sooner were the words out of her mouth when several shots were fired in the truck's direction. Bill grabbed his arm and groaned. Earl asked, "Did you get hit?"

Bill moaned. "No. I bumped my funny bone when I ducked down."

Sylvia saw the car parked in front of her. She could make out the silhouettes of several men. Thinking they might be more Whitecaps, she groaned. *What am I going to do now?*

Just as she neared the car, a herd of deer leaped in front of the truck. Sylvia swerved to avoid the deer and skidded into the ditch. Sylvia, Bill, and Earl jumped from the truck, ripped off their masks, and ran toward a stand of trees.

*   *   *   *

Wilbur saw the truck crash. He laughed gleefully. "We got 'em now. Stop here so we can follow them." Thirty men emerged from their vehicles and were about to give chase when they heard gunfire.

Gressley shouted, "That was a warning shot! Stay where you are."

A few men moved toward their cars. They stopped when another volley of shots was fired in their direction.

Gressley shouted again. "Damn it, don't move."

Sylvia peaked around a tree, and yelled, "John, we're over here! Wilbur Greene is chasing us."

Gressley shouted, "Wilbur Greene, stay where you are. I'm arresting you for the murder of Russell Wilcox."

Wilbur yelled, "You can't arrest me, detective. You have no jurisdiction out here."

One of the Whitecaps removed his mask. "Maybe he can't, but I can. I'm Lieutenant Barkheimer of the Michigan State Police." Three other state policemen removed their masks and pointed their revolvers at Wilbur and the other men. Barkheimer yelled to Gressley, "We came tonight to see what this group was up to. It's a good thing we did."

Gressley said, "Toby, you and Luke go explain to Lieutenant Barkheimer what the situation is. Oscar, come with me."

Gressley and Oscar Danbridge ran to the woods. Gressley yelled, "Sylvia, where are you? Are you OK?"

Sylvia emerged from the trees, tearing off the Whitecaps robe. "I'm just a little shaken, but I'll be all right in a few minutes."

Gressley swept Sylvia into his arms. "You scared me to death. I thought I was going to lose you. No more delays—I want to get married as soon as we can."

Holding on to him tightly, Sylvia whispered, "The sooner the better, my darling."

CHAPTER 42

▼

Sylvia Pointe and John Gressley were married the first Saturday in December. Sylvia's wish that the wedding take place at the Woman's Benefit Association was granted. Bina West stood with the other guests as the bride descended the magnificent stairs in the building's lobby. Sylvia wore an ankle-length white satin wedding gown with a beaded headband and a silk veil.

John smiled broadly at Sylvia. He wore a black frock coat, black cashmere trousers with a white stripe, and a double-breasted white waistcoat. John took Sylvia's hand as she reached the bottom of the stairs. Sylvia turned to stand beside John as the Reverend Tom Rossman of the Oaks Corner Methodist Church conducted the ceremony.

When the ceremony concluded, the newlyweds stood patiently in the receiving line. Afterward, guests took their places at tables in the large meeting room next to the lobby. Once everyone was seated, Toby Sharpe, who had served as best man, stood up. "It is a privilege and an honor to toast John and Sylvia today. They have been my friends and colleagues for seven years. I am happy they decided to get married, and I wish them well." Toby lifted a glass of Vernors Ginger Ale. "God bless Sylvia and John. For a special treat, I've asked Rachel Danbridge to sing 'A Pretty Girl is Like a Melody.'"

When Rachel finished singing, everyone cheered lustily. Edna Byrant, who shared a table with Bill Boyd and his uncle, said, "She has a beautiful voice."

Bill nodded in agreement. He also observed that Toby and Mary Sharpe had held hands and stared lovingly into each others' eyes during the song.

Edna said, "That was a beautiful ceremony—simple but elegant."

"I heard that John and Toby got promotions," said Clayton.

Bill said, "Effective January 1, 1920, it will be Lieutenant Gressley and Sergeant Sharpe. I can't think of two people in the department who are more deserving."

Clayton stood up and placed his hands on Bill's shoulder. "I see some old friends that I haven't talked to since my heart attack. You two enjoy the party."

Edna watched Clayton walk to the other side of the room. She said, "It's amazing that a policeman would be the ringleader in the Russell Wilcox's murder."

"Wilbur was convinced that Russell had stolen that car last summer. According to Weldon Clark, Wilbur talked the other three in helping him attack Russell. Weldon said that he thought they were just going to rough him up, and he was astonished when Russell was beaten to death."

Edna sighed. "It's terrible that people have that much hatred stored up."

Chris and Amanda Sharpe tapped Bill on the shoulder. Amanda squealed, "Hello, Big Bill."

Bill turned, "What are you two scamps doing?"

Chris said, "Nothing. We just want to say hi."

"Well, it's nice to see you. Have you met my friend?"

The two children shook their heads.

"This is Edna Bryant." Turning to Edna, he said, "And these two scallywags are Chris and Amanda Sharpe."

Edna said, "Pleased to meet you. Amanda, I saw your play, and I liked it a lot."

Amanda grinned. "Thanks."

Edna asked, "Do you want to be an actress when you grow up?"

"I want to be either an actress or an anthropologist."

Bill said, "Wow. Those are lofty goals." Turning to Chris, he asked, "How did your essay on the Underground Railroad turn out?"

"I got an A. Your uncle sure helped. Well, we've got to go now. It was nice meeting you, Miss Bryant."

"Nice meeting you, too." Edna watched the two children dash away. "You've known the Sharpes for a long time, haven't you?"

"Oh yes. Toby and I have been friends for twenty years. It was almost like I was part of their family before the war. But we've both been so busy since I got back; we haven't really seen each other very much."

"Thanks to your articles, he and John Gressley are certainly local heroes right now."

"Toby's idea of sending the fingerprints of Graham Hastings, alias Milton Burks, alias Benjamin Potts, alias who knows how many other names, to the IAI was brilliant. Hastings was arrested for interstate fraud."

Edna said, "There's one thing that isn't very clear. How did Toby become suspicious of Hastings in the first place?"

Bill leaned over and gave Edna a kiss. "I asked Toby the same thing, but he wouldn't answer. So I am afraid, my dear, that will remain a mystery."

Chronology of historical events

1919

- Harry and Bess Truman spent a portion of their honeymoon at the Harrington Hotel in Port Huron, Michigan. In the biography *Truman,* historian David McCullough wrote, "… that for Harry the very words 'Port Huron' would forever mean the ultimate in happiness."

- Max Schultze was the last of the twelve saboteurs who conspired to dynamite the St. Clair River Tunnel to be captured.

1920

- The Chicago American Giants won the first National Negro League championship.

- Henry Ford's weekly newspaper, *The Dearborn Independent,* published its first anti-Semitic article on May 22. The first article was titled "The International Jew: The World's Problem." For nearly two years, the paper continued its attack on Jews. Henry Ford made a public apology in 1927.

1921

- "Shoeless" Joe Jackson and seven of his Chicago White Sox teammates were banned from organized baseball for the rest of their lives for their association with gamblers during the 1919 World Series.

1924

- J. Edgar Hoover was placed in charge of the Justice Department's Bureau of Investigation, renamed the Federal Bureau of Investigation in 1935. He remained in that position until his death in 1972.

- Robert Evans was the first president of the Port Huron chapter of the NAACP.

1925

- The Ku Klux Klan had a membership estimated to be nearly four million throughout the United States. In that year, David Stephenson, Grand Dragon of the Realm of Indiana, was convicted of rape and murder. This and other revelations of criminal behavior, as well as internal bickering, led to a rapid decline in membership. By 1930, the number of members was down to approximately forty-five thousand.

1927

- After manufacturing nearly fourteen thousand automobiles, the Will Sainte Claire Motor Car Company closed. About eighty of these cars still exist.

1928

- Herbert Hoover was elected president of the United States.
- Dave Hanton opened his own shoe repair store. He died in 1959.

1929

- After being single for sixty-one years, Bina West married George Miller. She died in 1954.

1933

- Drinking alcohol became legal in the United States.

1937

- Smoking marijuana became illegal.

1947

- Jackie Robinson became the first African American to play Major League baseball since the Walker brothers in 1884.

1948

- Helen Floyd was the first African American teacher in the Port Huron public schools.

1955

- Michigan Agricultural College changed its name to Michigan State University of Agricultural and Applied Science. It became officially recognized as Michigan State University in 1964.

1969

- The Gratiot Inn was demolished.

- Joseph Moncrief became Port Huron's first African American policeman.

1973

- Springer and Rose clothing store closed.

1975

- The Grand Trunk Railroad Depot was demolished.

1976

- Audrey Pack became the first African American elected to the Port Huron city council. Nancy Maywar was her campaign manager.

1988

- Colleen Moore died. Between 1917 and 1934, she appeared in more than twenty films. She costarred with such famous actors as Tom Mix, Gary Cooper, and Spencer Tracy. Her Fairy Castle, an elaborate miniature palace, is on display at the Museum of Science and Industry in Chicago.

1998

- The Detroit Hudson's building, which eventually grew to twenty-five stories, was demolished.

Additional tidbits

- The Negro Leagues Committee of the Society for American Baseball Research has identified eleven Cuban players who debuted in the Major Leagues between 1911 and 1929 after having played on Negro League teams.

- No one was ever arrested for the 1889 lynching of Albert Martin.

- The Michigan vs. Ohio State football rivalry continues to be intense.

- Mueller Metals Company, now called Mueller Brass, is still in operation.

- Mount Olive Baptist Church still provides ministry in the Port Huron community.

Final notes

Everybody and everything mentioned in the following list was in Port Huron or Marysville in 1919: Jean Benini's Peek-a-Boo Burlesque Troupe; George Chambers; Helen Davidson; Family Theater; Farmer and Conselyea Shoe Store; Gratiot Inn; Grand Trunk Railroad Depot; Graziadei Orchestra; Dave Hanton; Harrington Hotel; Lakeside Cemetery; Majestic Theater; Maxine Theater; Reverend James Mayes; memorial to the soldiers of 1832; Mount Olive Baptist Church; Mueller's Metals Company; Clara Sibella; Governor Albert E. Sleeper; Springer and Rose clothing store; Bess Truman; Harry Truman; Bina West; C. Harold Wills; the Wills Sainte Claire Automobile Company; and the Woman's Benefit Association.

The Whitecaps of America terrorized several Midwestern communities in the late 1800s and early 1900s. Novelist Booth Tarkington exposed the organization's racist philosophy in his novel *The Gentleman from Indiana*. [*The Fiery Cross* by Wyn Craig Wade.]

Oaks Corner is fictional. Any resemblance between the fictional characters and anyone, living or dead, is purely coincidental. Some dates, times, and locations have been altered to facilitate the story.

978-0-595-42050-6
0-595-42050-8

Printed in the United States
80094LV00004B/160-186

9 780595 420506